How to Kill Friends and Eviscerate People

How to Kill Friends and Eviscerate People

BY

Jenny Johnston

WITH
Tim Paggi

PART 1

1

You Gotta Start Somewhere!

Have you ever wished you could stop competing with your coworkers, and just murder them instead?

I had that thought for the first time one day in 1996. The board and shareholders of the company where I worked contracted the services of a consultant who promised to "take the temperature" and "foster collaboration" among our five separate and siloed divisions. This particular meeting of our executive leadership team included me, as well as Cody MacMillan (Finance), Laird Ott (Operations Management), Philip Platt (Technology and Information Systems), and Hank Domino (Law). Also present was CEO Harold Rutberger—a man I once idolized—as well as the consultant, the only woman present besides myself, Senior Strategic Officer for the Nameless Corporation, Eva LeFey, who was tall and gaunt and had a face full of secrets.

I'll talk more about them later. For now, I'd like to focus on the most important subject: me. I had not yet acquired my famous supernatural powers, but as I went through the motions of several requisite, corporate teambuilding exercises, I gazed at my so-called colleagues with contempt. They listened to the consultant with such rapt attention, and whenever I made one of my witty jests or jabs, they refused to laugh.

I managed to stay awake throughout the brainstorming sessions. I forced myself to contribute to the compliment circle. But then Eva indicated that we all stand to "try something a little different."

"It's called a trust fall," she explained. "What I want you to do is stand up from your chairs, get into a line and then turn to your left. Good. Now, see the back of the head of the person in front of you? In the trust fall exercise, they will tip themselves backward, and the person behind catches them. Everyone got it?"

Starting with Laird, we went down the line one couple after the other, like a set of well-dressed dominoes. After being caught, they cried a satisfied laugh of relief. Two of them even high-fived and ended up with their arms around one another. Catching Philip was my job, and while I was able to prop the small man up, I cannot say that I escaped his salami-smelling armpits.

Then came my turn to trust.

I turned and shot a look at my catcher, Eva. While my heels add an inch or two, I stand around 5'8, and she was an imposing figure, at least six feet. If lacking in the personality department, she at least appeared very in shape, and I trusted her to catch me without difficulty. I scrunched my face at her, then looked forward and let myself fall back into whatever mysterious air lay out of view, behind me.

It felt quite liberating, letting myself go. I'd never done that before, and in fact my arms flew to my sides. Time slowed, my coworkers evaporated, and my eyes concentrated on the drop ceiling above, whose pock marks were like a collection of interstellar phenomena in an endless gray universe. I fell and fell, blissful, until I realized I still fell. And I kept falling, Dear Reader, down and down as if a vortex had opened in the center of the conference room floor.

Then I crashed on the carpet. Eva apologized, professing that she was not ready, but her face told the truth: she was *delighted* that I fell to the floor. They all were! The others snickered and giggled for the first time that day, not with me but *at* me. "Oh boy, quite the spill there, Jenny!"

"That's gonna leave a mark, ha!"

Harold, the CEO and my only ally, helped me to my feet. I thanked him but glared at the others, wishing that I could ditch the masquerade of professionalism and chew them out. I knew Eva let me drop on purpose. I knew that they all watched with amusement as she stepped aside, that they collectively chose to not warn me. They were a confederacy, one that had gathered arms against me, and for the first time, I wished to see them dead.

That's when it all started.

But Why Should You Listen to Me?

My name is Jenny Johnston. I've worked in the professional sphere from 1984 to just earlier this year, 1997. Along the way, I worked as a high-level executive and eventually appointed myself CEO of KLR, Inc., briefly, in 1996. I resigned from that position to start my own firm, and now assist Fortune 100 companies scale down their operations. In addition, I of course commune with N'thodylarp, AKA It That Tends the Gateways to Abomination.

That might sound impressive, because it is. I'm rich, famous, and possess a control over the dark arts that you wouldn't believe, but I should tell you that I started as just a regular gal, growing up in the small town of Lutherville, Maryland (outside of Baltimore). I was a child of the 50's: three channels on the black and white TV, three flavors of ice cream, and zero complaints. As far as I knew, a simple life was just perfect.

Dear Reader, I don't care your age, your race, or what furry parts reside in your underwear. I don't care if you're rich, poor, talented or feeble-minded. The principles outlined in this volume apply equally to all human beings, including you. You plucked this book off the shelf of your local Barnes and Noble or Waldenbooks for a reason. That simple act of purchasing my book will, I guarantee, become the most impactful action of your life, because it was your first step on the path to stop working and start killing.

You're probably saying to yourself, hold on! Did she say *stop working*?

Yes, I did. But I don't mean quit your job. I repeat: Do. Not. Quit. Your. Job. That would be a grievous misinterpretation of my message. Confused? Don't worry, I was too, once. It's a tricky concept, and hey, that's why I wrote a whole book about it.

For now, listen: you must go to work, but must not, under any circumstance, *do* work at work. You must not fall prey to the traps and pitfalls placed upon you by society's expectations. In other words...

You Must Not Succumb to "Work Brain" Mentality

What I stress to my clients is that neither your accomplishments nor the quality of your performance matters one iota. Nobody cares. You receive no bonus points. God keeps no tally of your completed tasks. I've witnessed an endless procession of kings and clowns sacrifice their sanity for their labors, and all that amounts from it is that each and every one of them turn into what I call "Work Brains."

Work Brains show up early. They return phone calls ASAP. They roll up their sleeves and scrub the counters clean. They execute each bullet point on their job description and then—get this—they do *even more* than instructed, with absolutely no reward in sight! Work Brains supervise and train their staff, and they refrain from banishing others' souls into the depths of cosmic netherworlds beyond human comprehension.

Work Brain syndrome can strike any American at any time. There's a good chance that you yourself suffer from this condition. Do any of the following symptoms sound familiar?

- **Seeking feedback or approval from managers or subordinates**
- **Needing desperately to fit in among crowds of average, Work-Brained dunces**
- **Believing in vague, undefined systems promising material/spiritual rewards for hard work**

Heck, in most cases, productivity only complicates your life for the worse. You will be expected to reproduce your success again and again, to higher and higher degrees, until it becomes impossible, and the mob shuns you in favor of the next leader. Eventually, your compatriots will crucify you for your perceived shortcomings.

If you doubt that what I say is true, then I want you to take a moment to visualize your own workplace. Are the best, smartest people in charge? Do others notice and applaud when you accomplish your goals on time?

According to a survey conducted by Johnston Research in 1997, employees who reported that they did more than what was asked of them were 78% more likely to be disgruntled in their workplace. When asked, many admitted resorting to Prozac, therapy, or church.

Meanwhile, the employees who actively shirked their responsibilities in favor of pursuing random whims were a whopping 92% more likely to feel appreciated.

Let's examine a case study. My client worked for the legal firm, Pembroke and Shea. She was an associate who couldn't get ahead no matter how hard she tried. When I materialized into her office, I introduced myself but said little else. This is normal. I instructed the Associate to go about her business and allow me to observe her daily routine, urging her to do more or less what she did at work. She reluctantly agreed, though my arrival confused her. "I didn't hear you come in," she remarked. "And nobody's informed me that we'd hired consultants."

I'm not sure how much I clarified by informing her nobody hires me. *I* choose my clients.

Now her whole life, she'd done everything right. Harvard cum laude, now a prosecutor in a top corporate firm. She had an ingrained habit of staying late, poring over legal documents, making calls, and drafting effective, unexpected lines against the defense. I witnessed her spend an entire evening reviewing tax law, then watched with bemused shock as she listened to a client patiently and attentively, making notes of important points throughout their discussion.

Later, the two of us sat down with a couple Cherry Coca-Cola's. I asked what she wanted out of her career, and she said, "To make partner, of course!"

"Honey," I said...

"You'll Never Climb Another Rung Up That Ladder with That Heavy Sack of Chores Strapped to Your Back."

Hearing that, she cried. She protested. She tried convincing me that Law is some higher calling requiring special precision and blah, blah, blah. People always turn into hound dogs when I deliver the news, because their Work Brain mentality has ingrained itself deep enough that it's become a symbiotic parasite.

I told her it was her own life, and she could squander it as she pleased, but asked her to implement my suggestions for one week only. If she didn't have significantly more power by the end of one week—five business days, really— then I would pack up my bags and scram. My bossiness bothered her, but I didn't care. In fact, I don't care about anything, least of all the feelings of others.

That week, instead of her old routine, she would do the new. Together, we charted out the principal partners and associates who were holding her back, and even included brackets for high-ranking paralegals and other collaborators who represented opposition. Then we set about our work.

As usual, I provided a demonstration of what she'd eventually be doing herself. "I can work wonders on anyone, anywhere," I informed my timorous client. We didn't even need to be in the same room as our victim.

We targeted a principal in a corner office. We went to the adjacent office, where I convinced its occupant to get lost. Then I told my client to put her ear to the wall and listen. "What do you hear?" I asked.

"Nothing much," she said with an uncertain frown.

"Go on," I said. "Listen again."

She set her ear upon the eggshell-colored wall once more, and I watched her face become more and more inquisitive, listening to the events befalling the partner in the next room. "Gurgling," she said, confused. "Like a water fountain? But the pressure's weak and it's just making a bunch of bubbles...and sputtering."

Beneath her executive power suit, she trembled like a leaf in a gentle breeze. The next look she gave me was a potpourri of confusion and terror. "Who are you?" she asked, voice threatening to erupt into a scream. "Oh God, oh God, why is this happening? What are you doing to him?"

A fair question, and she really wanted to know. So, using the power of my mind, I opened a window in the dividing wall to reveal the effects of my work. What I did to the man in the next office was rather commonplace in my opinion but would take a cleaning crew weeks to get rid of completely.

Though the spirit of a killing can never be erased...

And I'm not sure how salvageable the carpet was, covered with such an impressive array of entrails.

High-ranking professionals often prove naïve. In the lawyer's case, she could not conceive how, without lifting a finger, I turned a man inside-out and painted the walls and ceilings with his guts. She assumed a certain set of laws dictated how the natural world's functions, and she viewed existence through a false veil of sanity. What I demonstrated is that no one is safe. Reality's integrity is never guaranteed. The millennium is turning, the old world is dying, and the angel of death casts her shadow across all human endeavors, indifferent to logic or reason.

And Dear Reader...

If You're a Little Confused

...that's okay, because the information I'm bringing you is new and possibly scary. But I will explain myself in full. More importantly, of course, by allowing the words upon these pages to impress themselves through your eyes and upon your mind, you will become a ruthless sorcerer or sorceress capable of exacting supernatural torment.

Now, we are almost set to begin. But first, I need you to promise two things:

1. Your trust

Yes, you must believe that every word I tell you is true. You will even be able to prove it by the time you finish the book (which will be upon you sooner than you think). You may feel a little unmoored by my unconventional narrative, but this is essential for my purposes. Trust me: an ah-ha moment is coming (as well as a few AHHH AHHH moments).

2. Your attention

To transform your dreary life, I require your entire focus and dedication to this book's teachings. It may be necessary to pause after each chapter, reflect, take notes, and even re-read to truly absorb what I'm telling you.

Sound good? Then, Dear Reader, take my hand, and allow me to transport you three years into the past yet again, back to the year 1996, when I was still just a normal, forty-two-year-old woman with a normal job, a normal family and a normal home, in the suburbs of Baltimore still trying to figure out just how best to eradicate my associates.

2

THE QUEEN BEE OF THE WORK BRAINS

KLR's founder and original CEO, Byron Ludlow, was ousted in 1985, and the board voted in Harold Rutberger, a regional mover and shaker who would become my professional mentor. Under Harold's guidance, the company finally loosened its depression-era policies and adapted to the times.

Harold's first big move was to relocate the headquarters, which Ludlow ran out of a poorly maintained historical structure three blocks north of Baltimore's famed Inner Harbor. Harold moved KLR to a glass and steel mid-rise in the suburbs and traded out the austere metal desks for shiny wooden ones. He introduced posh corporate flavor and brought his frat house style to meetings. "Business isn't done at a desk," he advised rookie salesmen at their orientation happy hours. "It's done in the sports bar!"

Harold brought me on in 1991. According to him, he hired me as a head of Product Services for my personality alone. "You don't bore me," he confided, two neat whiskeys into our first luncheon. "That's the most essential quality I look for in any employee. That and something special about you, which is your big imagination."

He lavished upon me a company car and Amex. He encouraged me to wine and dine potential suppliers and manufacturers, and to delegate the bookkeeping nitty-gritty to my division's underlings. Business plateaued, but somehow profits soared. After seven years in middle management and dead-end supervisory roles, I finally found my place in the world. Of course, in reality...

THERE IS NO PLACE FOR YOU

...in this or any other world. Eventually, the corporate waters shift, and we humans get caught up in the riptides. What had once been the new guard swapped out for a slew of business-minded professionals and self-stylized gurus, bringing with them a host of technological nonsense and New Age enlightenment. They had ponytails and drove foreign cars and infested our operations like groundhogs in a field of clover.

Harold became embroiled in a legal dispute with his wife, and this sapped him of his bravado. He caved when leadership voted to stop providing "undeserved" bonuses and "opulent" company cars. I'll never forget the morning they sent a hulking tow-truck to my house and dragged away my lime-green Mercedes like it was some rusting hot rod beside a trailer.

Dear Reader: I wept. For a humiliating two weeks, I resorted to driving the ol' family van to go between my house, my work, and my favorite mall.

Then things got tense.

Hostile, even. My lunches often disappeared from the

fridge. One day, I sat in my office chair only to find that it was unscrewed, and it collapsed beneath me. At meetings, they routinely cut me off whenever I tried to contribute or point to my sales numbers. Whenever I brought printouts and an easel for presentations, the new tech guru Philip Platt snickered and insisted I try some dread-inducing program called PowerPoint.

All that I could think to do to stab back at them was to outwork those Work Brains! For months, I endeavored to:

- **do a good job**
- **follow the rules**
- **be a good girl**
- **be viewed as smart and capable**

...and to those ends, arrived at meetings with pre-written talking points detailing my past week's accomplishments, as well as my short- and long-term objectives. I often volunteered for presentations on ancillary topics and compiled key metric reports. Doubling down, I arrived early and stayed late. I attended professional development trainings and trade shows. I even won several awards for regional commerce, including the Baltimore County Association for Working Women's annual *Businesswoman of the Year Award*.

WHERE DID ALL THIS WORKITY-WORK GET ME?

Just one step closer to the grave.

My hunch that the dunces had joined in confederacy against me was confirmed on that fateful day of the trust fall, when Eva LeFey led their most blatant workplace prank.

Afterward, I still felt sore (figuratively and literally). When the division heads all cleared out, heading back to their bastions, only Harold remained. We sat together at a corner of the long conference table. The sky outside thick-ened with dirty clouds, and the steel light through the many windows cast a ghostly, foreboding mantle.

I asked Harold outright, "What's going on around here? This crew makes it impossible to get reimbursed for client dinners, or get vacations covered. That's not even mention-ing the actual work, which is getting out of hand. Last week, Cody asked for some figures sent to him in an email. Harold, do you hear me? An *email*."

With a sigh, he formed a tent with his massive fingers and rested his face upon it. Awkward silence followed so I looked around as a bolt of heat lightning illuminated the suburbs outside. The conference room featured few deco-rations, though standing upon an end table was a bust of Byron Ludlow. Harold had commissioned it because Harold had a special interest in lifelike, bronze sculpture—an art form I find off-putting. He'd also had one done of his politi-cal idol, Ronald Reagan, and its cheery, all-American figure proudly waved to greet all who entered through the impec-cably shined glass doors of KLR.

"Things have gotten away from me, I'll admit," Harold finally said.

"*Gotten away* from you? They're making a mockery of this place! Last week they vetoed petty cash, and today, that dirty consultant watched me fall, didn't she? Didn't she?"

Harold pulled himself up. He was in every way large, clean shaven, and very bald on his pate. As CEO, he had access to more information than I did, but for propriety's sake couldn't outright admit the consultant and our high-est-ranking staff were also mutineers.

He nodded soberly and whispered. "Jenny, I shouldn't tell this to you yet, but big change is coming. You know the shareholder quarterly in two weeks?"

"What about it?"

"A restructure will be discussed then. That's why the folks from Nameless are popping up, including Eva. I tried shooting it down but was outvoted."

"You think they're gonna edge us two out?"

He gave me the *who knows* shrug, and I wondered into which shadowy wastebin had our halcyon days been tossed? Here was the man who had shown me that work was about more than your duties; it was a lifestyle, a playground for type-A adults. It saddened me to see Harold long faced and speechless.

Then he did a curious thing. Without looking at me, he rested his chilly left hand upon mine. Our two wedding bands made a tiny clink. My cheeks flushed, and my upper arms blossomed in goose bumps. He asked, "We're in this together, right?"

Inspired, I nodded.

"Good, I need you," he said with two raps of his knuckles upon the table. Within him, the mighty Harold of yesterday suddenly glowed anew. "These hot shots forgot who they're messing with! I've got connections, and I'm going to introduce you. What do you say, will you be my plus-one next Thursday at the BDC Society?"

I nearly gasped and released my hands from his. Whispers of the downtown BDC Society meetings were heard throughout every business in our region, but they were impossibly exclusive, only attended by moguls, lawyers and politicians. If Harold had access to these types, he may have been plotting counter measures.

The prospect thrilled me to the edge of terror. Nonetheless, I told him, "Yes. Definitely."

"Good, good," he said. He checked his platinum Rolex, then stood. "I'm all booked up the rest of this week, so

I won't be able to talk until then. In the meantime, I need you to do something important with that big imagination of yours, Jenny. Daydream up a plan for what we're going to do, got it? I want something they won't see coming—something creative."

I knew his candle burned at both ends and he lacked the brain space to elaborate on what kind of plan, but oh, how creative I would become.

But that was still all in good time. For now, I needed to process my thoughts and emotions, and to do that, I always say...

Use Good Assistants!

Whenever I meet someone just getting started in their career, I tell them the same thing. *You need to get people underneath you as soon as possible.*

Humans are impressed by power. If you aren't bossing people around, then you'll never attract attention from the power brokers in your life. Does successful leadership require any special skills? No. All you need is to start telling others what to do. If they fail, then you either cut them off, fire them or murder them. Most people, however, will eventually fall in line.

For my part, a whole department looked up to me: three tiers of salespeople, their assistants, a graphic designer and two accountants filled the third-floor cubicles and offices. I cared not what any of them did with their time. If they showed up, did as I said, and never under any circumstance brought me bad news, I left them to their own devices.

Only one of my employees mattered.

Meet my assistant, Lance. As I marched into my suite, back from the team building fiasco, I found Lance with his oxfords resting on his desk outside my office. Lance was flippant, but perceived my emotional states well, and no doubt read the turmoil written across my face.

"You must tell me what mischief is brewing," he said, slipping into my office and shutting the door behind him. "There's something going on and I want in!"

Fast forward to thirty minutes later, when we sat in the smoking section of the York Road Wendy's, openly gossiping like the hairdressers at Sally's Stylez. Through the window, we saw the parking lot, and beyond it the ongoing stream of traffic, as well as a Mobile, an Exxon, a McDonald's and a Pizza Hut. Halfway through our hamburgers, I decided to get to the meat of our lunch date. "The other division heads are plotting against me," I said. "And it's freakin' depressing."

HOT TIPS

1. Never display weakness to a higher up or equal, but underlings will always hand over their trust if you confide in them.

2. If your job does not yet provide emotional support assistants, there are plenty of waiters, baristas and store managers required to provide free therapy to you as part of their job!

Lance wiped some ketchup from the side of his mouth. He was a good-looking young man. From his coiffed 'do to his elaborate ensembles (today's looked like something out of Gentleman's Quarterly), I took Lance to be both independently wealthy and gay. We never broached the topic, but if he ever felt comfortable enough to come out, I'd give him my full support. After all, it's a free country, and he was technically my best friend. Still in his twenties, Lance was a hopeless secretary, but I couldn't care less. He was an avid gossip-fiend and a prominent figure in the KLR whisper network that included other assistants, middle managers, outliers and even janitors. Lance always insisted they had the real dirt.

"I have it on good authority," he began, "that many see the company as rudderless under Harold's command. The shareholders might be plotting a big surprise."

Sometimes higher-ups fed bad information to the spiderweb to see how it would play further down the line, but what Lance told me was true, according to Harold. I decided to feed a juicy detail back into his gossip channel. "It's a restructure, probably with the Nameless Corporation. They might be planning to swap a few pieces on the chess board."

"Sounds bad," Lance fretted. "Jenny, if I get fired, I'll need to get a job at some dirty place like a gas station, or a public school. I'd kill myself!"

I blanked out for a moment, picturing my own fate: sitting at home, drinking wine, and eventually succumbing to the siren calls of the other neighborhood housewives by taking up tennis.

Yes, I decided right there and then. All of them—the shareholders, board, consultants and two-timing division heads—all needed to be stopped. Especially the one who dropped me. "Lance, have you heard anything about Eva?"

He nodded. "Yes, my sources dished big about her, and it's important. But I'm not going to just tell you. Not without..."

I finished chewing some fries and brushed the sandy salt off my fingers, then attempted to wipe them clean with a flimsy paper napkin. I knew what Lance wanted, so I craned my neck around to study today's Wendy's clerks. Didn't look too tough, but I couldn't remember if we'd had them recently. "Really? Again?"

He flashed me a mischievous grin. "You know you want to."

I needed a prop and chose my half-full medium Diet Coke. I strutted out of the smoking section and, ignoring the line of customers, cut to the front while rattling my cup. "Excuse me?" I said to the mid-twenties' girl in a red shirt and hat behind the register.

She gave me some kind of look. Perhaps Lance and I had, in fact, recently attended the establishment. Regardless, I had to raise my voice for Lance to hear from where he sat, which meant that everyone else in the restaurant probably heard too. "My Coke came with barely any ice," I complained. "Could you?"

I popped off the plastic lid and handed it to her, a little sticky liquid spilling over the side. She hesitated in a moment of personal quandary, then took my cup and filled it to the tippy top with ice. This was her small act of spite, and when she reached across the counter to hand it back, I just folded my arms and let her hold it, all the while as new customers entered. "*That's* too much," I said. "What I want, miss, is the right amount—the Goldilocks amount."

Seeing her squirm delighted me, and Lance as well, whose barely contained laughter sounded more akin to violent choking. The cashier looked annoyed, which meant I had her right where I wanted her. When she rolled her eyes, I struck.

"I don't appreciate your attitude," I said. "So I'm going to need to speak with your manager."

•

Five minutes and one refund later, the two of us stumbled out of the joint high on power, with all eyes inside no doubt following us back to my lowly family van. We took our seats but kept open the doors, and I lit two more Virginia Slims. "Good enough?" I asked. "Did that satisfy your sick desires?"

"I honestly don't know how you can do that," he said between laughs, wiping his face dry with his free hand. "I'd die. You have a gift, Jenny."

"Now that it's out of the way, dish on Eva."

He took a long puff, gazing out over the many lanes of traffic, then ashed onto the asphalt. At first, I wondered why he stalled on answering, then realized he was trying to calm down and change his mood. What he had to tell me looked serious. "This I've heard from two sources. You need to be careful around Eva. She's not like other employees."

"Dude, none of that is helpful. Not even, like, a little."

"They say she's *dangerous*."

I squinted. "Well, she did let me drop, if that's what you mean. Wait, what do you mean?"

Even though it was just the two us, Lance lowered his voice to a conspiratorial whisper. "They say she has powers. She can do things with her mind."

At the time, this sounded like lunacy. I searched his eyes for signs of madness or jest, and finding neither, informed him he still owed me some real dirt, fast.

To our right, the cashier stormed out of Wendy's toward her car. The manager followed, begging her to stay. I made out what the clerk shouted back to him. "Screw this place! I'm out of here."

Her words dislodged a creative block for me as far as a Big Idea for Harold. It came to me all at once: we shouldn't try to save the company.

No, we should take the biggest clients and start our own company—together!

Lance and his conspiracies dissolved as I leaned my head back into the van's cushy seat, images of the division heads' jealousy dancing through my mind. I pictured them stewing in a big meeting, looking hungover after learning the legacy clients flocked our direction. Just like the nearby scene, I imagined them hemorrhaging employees and begging them not to quit. I imagined them groveling at consultants like Eva, spending millions just to be told how to right the ship.

And I imagined the not-too-distant Friday afternoon when, due to nothing but their own hubris, the final staff cleared their belongings and exited to the parking lot, before the debtors padlocked everything, and the doors of KLR, Inc. closed for good.

But to succeed at this beautiful plan, I'd need to get Harold on my side. I dropped Lance back at HQ, then drove first to the bank, where my lender explained how much cash I could take out. It wouldn't be enough. Then I asked about their second mortgage packages.

Later, an associate told me, "And of course, we'll require Mr. Johnston's signature on the paperwork, as well."

"Of course," I replied. That was easy enough to fake.

My proposal to Harold would appeal not only to his brain, but to his heart. But it wouldn't come cheap. As a token of my sincerity, I called an artist and commissioned a bronze sculpture of the two of us side by side in our power suits, confidently striding forward.

I wanted it small, *like a paperweight*, I explained. *But full of realistic detail.* Our clothes and our faces and everything needed to really look like us. For reference, I gave the sculptor multiple photographs. When Harold saw how much I wanted to begin a new venture, he'd know that he made the right choice aligning with me. Say what you will about me, but I'm a fighter. And with a plan like this, what could possibly go wrong?

3

PREPARE FOR SURPRISES

The next week passed in anxiety-drenched days and sleepless nights. The Thursday of the downtown BDC meeting finally arrived, and Harold said he'd swing by around seven to pick me up. My husband John was away on business, and our daughter Catherine claimed to be entirely self-reliant and indifferent to my company. She would probably head out to "the movies" or some other social gathering which she'd insist was of an academic nature, if I'd asked.

I couldn't eat and my guts felt twisty. To kill time, I strolled around my neighborhood, a gated community of standalone homes called Valley Fields. The groundskeepers had mowed that day, so I avoided the lawn and instead headed down my driveway to the sidewalk, surrounded by birdsong and the not-so-distant rush of ongoing highway traffic.

Everything filled me with profound irritation. I hated how my neighbor's guests parked near the edge of our lawn. I hated how another neighbor's braying dogs ruined the ambiance. And I hated how those across the street from me simply repainted their house a terrible shade of beige without first consulting the HOA. Seriously, it looked like a big cardboard box with a Benz outside.

It's almost unfair how easy and effortless my life had become. At some point, my days just became full of soft couch cushions, natural skin creams, and whatever I could dream of to eat. All this comfort—all this stuff—left me feeling empty inside. Besides the untimely death of my sister, I'd never faced any real hardship.

That is not to underplay the effect her death had on my life. My sister died in a freak diving accident when I was sixteen, yet her presence always weighed heavily on me. Her name was Carol and she was two years older. She was tall and her hair was a pure flaxen blonde, not the dirty, cheap knock-off blonde I'd been born with. Something about her effortless good looks and guiltless demeanor instantly earned the respect of all who met her. Our friends and family came to expect so much from her that they'd plain forgotten to expect anything from me, and I'd spent the better part of my childhood in her shadow. From the sidelines, I watched as she placed second in the state spelling bee; I clapped mirthlessly in the bleachers as she beat out Tracy Islington to take the gold trophy in the regional tennis championship. I sat through so many family dinners listening to Mom and Dad direct all their love at her, and I answered dozens of phone calls, as if I was her secretary, from her many handsome, well-positioned suitors.

I'd been present when she died, too, at the edge of Prettyboy Reservoir. She shouldn't have jumped over that day, everyone agreed. That she hit the rock and not the water surprised everyone, considering her athletic prowess and knack for precision. The paramedics came to clean her up, and I'll never forget the scratchy, obligatory blanket they wrapped around my sixteen-year-old self, curled up in the woods with my knees up to my chest, sobbing.

Still ambling through my neighborhood and lost in thought, I turned to look at my large house, there atop its modest hill. All that had been a long time ago, and I needed to drop Carol's memory. I tried convincing myself that I'd succeeded quite nicely. I had a good-looking, successful husband and we were rich. Who knows—if Carol had been able to age alongside me, it's possible I'd have outpaced her success-wise. And yet...and yet...because she died so young, her absence formed a gargantuan void that blotted out all my so-called successes. Carol's tragic passing superseded all I'd ever become to the eyes of my friends and family, and even to myself.

Still gazing at my house from a distance, I decided that this pain must serve a purpose, that it made me a person of a higher calling. If I was able to convince a man of Harold's stature to break from KLR to start a visionary company with me, would I finally, at the overripe age of forty-two, fill The Emptiness inside me and become my own person? Yes. Yes, I would.

But I needed things to work with Harold.

Two minutes later, his Lincoln Navigator pulled up beside me. "Looking for a good time?" he asked through the rolled-down window. Being pulled from my gloomy thoughts pleased me, and looking at his big, grinning face, I convinced myself that he was the antidote to my life's challenges and shortcomings.

Another thing: Harold and I had slept together. Only once, two years prior, but it happened. Other than that, his interest in me has remained 100% professional. And to be clear, he didn't make the pass. Not exactly. He was the special kind of man who used his power not to coerce women but to surround himself with them, and then demonstrate his power. By the way his smiles always lingered, and how he gently—yet persistently—placed his hand upon the small of my back as I passed through a doorway, I knew that if I expressed any interest, he would allow me to step into his lure. And that's what I did, one night after dinner at a conference in Bethesda. I never asked if he admitted it to Donna, but I certainly never told John.

I gazed out the window as we shot down I-83, the wooded suburbs giving away first to the sparse neighborhoods of Baltimore's outer regions, before being surrounded within minutes by the tall buildings of its denser, dirtier urban core. Harold pulled off the interstate and navigated some winding streets enroute to a glittering hotel overlooking the city's harbor. As we got out and walked to the soiree, Harold never questioned why I'd brought my large purse, which contained my business proposal and the beautiful sculpture, which I'd picked up just in the nick of time during my lunchbreak.

Once inside, I spotted recognizable politicians like mayor Carl Smoke, and local businessmen like Jeff Paterassis, the bakery magnate. There weren't many women, and as I sipped a peachy champagne served by a tuxedoed waiter, I wondered if Harold brought me along as mere arm candy.

After a couple hours, Harold and I passed one another in the crowd, and he suggested we leave. As we walked through the cavernous parking garage, I felt proud of the several business cards I'd acquired but wondered why he'd bothered bringing me. He'd acted aloof all night, introducing me only as *my colleague Jenny* and nothing more. Worse, he stumbled from too many scotches on our way out.

He turned up the radio as we sped through the city streets, flooding his car with an obnoxious pop song he claimed to love, featuring a group of young women proclaiming their rules about being lovers and friends. He also wanted to talk, so both of us needed to shout to be heard over the music.

As I've said, I'd been to more than a few conferences and galas with him and knew drinking got him surly, but tonight was worse. He incoherently speechified about some deal gone wrong, and all the while I debated delaying my plan until another day. But the sculpture had cost me thousands and I felt anxious to reveal it.

So caught up, I failed to notice that we had departed from the comparably clean downtown area with its banks and chain restaurants and found ourselves in a run-down part of town. On either side of the streets stood damaged homes, on whose stoops congregated suspicious-looking people. My parents once lived in such a neighborhood but moved and never returned. They often spoke with scorn of what had become of the city after they—as well as their peers—fled for the suburb's greener pastures.

The bleakness unnerved me. I saw no maintained parks, garbage littered the streets and sidewalks, and the only stores were liquor stores. Some of the houses were completely vacant, as if they'd had a fire or partial demolition. Their roofs were gone, and their windows were full of broken glass through which I spied scraggly trees and the sky.

"This isn't the way we came," I commented, but I don't think Harold heard. He kept singing along with his song like it was some sea shanty. I twisted down the volume knob. "Listen you asked for a proposal, remember? I have one."

"Oooh, a proposal!" he said with a belly laugh. As he lit a cigarette, he removed his hands from the wheel and his focus from the road. The car swerved between lanes and *ka-chunked* over a nasty pothole. "What's Jenny thinking about proposing?"

"You know as well as I do, Harold," I said, cutting to the chase. "The other division heads mock this company. I have reason to believe they're planning a takeover with Eva, and they want to take both of us down!"

He laughed at that, though it carried no merriment. It was a belligerent, hectoring laugh that rattled the car's interior. "You think I don't know that?" he shouted as we raced faster. Without warning, Harold slammed into a sharp right turn down a one-way street, and I gripped the door handle so that my head wouldn't smash into his shoulder. The SUV's right side hit the curb and scraped along a stop sign.

One side of our current street was an old stone wall, atop which was set an imposing, barbed wire fence. Abandoned homes populated the street's other side. It occurred to me then that this drive was much like the late stage of Harold's career at KLR: no direction and losing control in a vessel of luxury. I needed to calm him, to focus him, and only one thing would do the trick.

"Harold, I have a gift for you."

Hearing my promise, he actually stopped ranting and let off the gas a little. I reached into my bag and placed my hand around the sculpture. Showing it to him would snap him back to reality. "A gift?" he murmured, gaze falling to the side and regarding me with a sudden onset of clarity. "Jenny, you didn't need to give me a gift."

This was the kind of moment people live for. Just as I pulled the sculpture from within my bag, so too did I pull deeply from my hidden well of courage. How my heart swelled, knowing that once he saw my magnanimous gesture—the artistic symbol of my dedication—he'd be so touched he'd get on board with my plan, and together we'd conquer the—

Smash.

Crack.

At some point in the last minute, both of us stopped watching the road, and it was evident we'd run into something big...and then run it over. Harold slammed the brakes and my lap suddenly felt much lighter. Something happened to the sculpture, but I didn't care what. My instinct immediately turned me around, and I stared through the SUV's rear windshield, trying to see what we'd hit.

In the center of the otherwise deserted street, illuminated beneath the cone of a streetlight's milky glare, lay a lumpy, motionless pile.

Well, not completely motionless. The pile twitched just a little bit. And it leaked.

Without looking away, I reached and tapped on the sleeve of Harold's sports coat. "W-w-we need to get out."

He apparently had the opposite thought, and the car crawled up the street at an indecisive pace.

"Harold, for Chrissakes, stop the car. I think you hit somebody," I said, words barely passing my trembling lips.

"Don't tell me *I* hit somebody," he insisted, nasty and very defensive. "You're the one who decided to distract me with, with...whatever the hell that is."

I sat back in my seat and took a moment to observe how, when we'd abruptly stopped, the sculpture had flung loose from my hands and smacked straight into the windshield. It currently remained lodged in it by bronze likenesses of our two heads, both of which had penetrated the glass. My shock and sadness at this sight were erased by the possibility of our having killed whoever lay back there in the street.

Harold pulled over at a haphazard angle and stared into space, his body bolt upright and painfully rigid. No cars or bystanders were nearby, but that didn't stop the uncanny sensation of being watched, as if hidden observers spied our actions from the gaping windows of the shuttered homes. "We're not stopping," Harold said, resigned. "It doesn't matter that we hit somebody. That somebody...is nobody. If we call the police or an ambulance, it won't change the fact that we hit them. We can't help."

I started to cry. I'd been on a lot of drunken car rides with men, and a few fender benders too. But I'd never actually collided with someone's body at full speed, and I finally pried my eyes from the shadow at the center of the street, now half a block behind us. "We should check to see if they need help," I said, sniffling.

"Help them how? Are you a doctor? Do you have George Clooney's number at the ER?"

"Then we should drive to the nearest payphone!" I exclaimed, having no idea where we were or what we were near. As far as I was concerned, we'd somehow taken a route that transported us out of the United States and into some foreboding third world country.

"It doesn't matter. Killing someone doesn't matter like you think it does. So I'm taking you home, then going home myself to get some sleep."

Dear Reader, Remember...

...that I was still in the grips of the dreaded Work Brain, and still also believed in the existence of law enforcement. Driving away from a hit and run might result in significant legal troubles, and the threat of a women's prison with all its associated taboos and stigmas compelled me to insist to Harold, "No, no. Back up. We must check on....it. It might still be alive."

He'd wanted me to agree, and therefore give him permission to abscond. I didn't give it to him, and now he needed to face the music. In sixty seconds, he'd gone from the high-highs of his Thursday evening revelries to the low-lows of tomorrow's hangover, and his face sunk into something haggard and grim. Since still no other cars drove down this quiet street, he maneuvered backwards and halted once we approached, hitting the hazards.

I exited first and he followed.

Once outside, the street's desolation hit harder. We were like the sole passengers on a haunted house carnival ride, forced to disembark and explore the surrounding phantasmagoria. Dogs yowled and sirens wailed in the distance. What sounded like a tin can scraped against concrete somewhere close, and the far-off toot of what must have been a train added a mournful note. Undercutting the humid air was a uric tang like cheap wine gone bad and the vegetal odor of the jungly weeds overtaking the urban ruins. With tears and snot streaming from my face, I approached the fallen body.

We'd hit a black man. We'd hit him so hard that the impact projected him backward onto the asphalt, before both left tires crushed over his chest. Some twitchy movement remained in his neck and right arm, but he was a goner. Even if he somehow could have been put on life support, he'd surely choose death. Anyone would. All his vital organs were smashed into a wet, meaty pulp, and his ribs stabbed out from beneath his skin. Obscene amounts of blood pooled everywhere and trickled into the road's cracks. His head was bent at a right angle, and his fluttery eyes stared at a random clump of dandelions as if their jaundiced crowns contained the secret meaning of life.

Our current environment didn't exactly invite any well-meaning cry for help. I'd seen plenty of tough-looking characters on the surrounding blocks and didn't know if I trusted them not to mug us. "Okay, okay," I said, gathering composure. "Let's go find a gas station—"

Transfixed by the dying man, Harold didn't reply and staggered back toward the car. Unsure what else to do, I followed. That's when I confirmed for the first time that we were not alone.

About twenty paces up the street, a door to one of the abandoned rowhomes opened, and a woman stepped out onto its cracked stoop. Whether she'd witnessed the entire scene, or only the bloody aftermath, she watched us now.

Incongruous in my high heels and hoop earrings, I rushed her direction for assistance. I didn't realize that Harold chased after me until he grabbed my arm and yanked me back violently. "Come on!" he spat in my ear. "We're leaving."

I grabbed his coat to keep my footing. As he dragged me a couple stumbling steps, I twisted my neck around to glance the woman. It astonished me that she'd closed half the distance between us, now standing in the center of the road. Though the streetlight above flickered, I saw in its intermittent bursts that she was white, very old and frail, and wore a dirty, multi-colored shawl that appeared handmade. How had a woman her age moved so quickly?

She opened her mouth, revealing an incomplete set of teeth.

"Who do you worship?"

Her gravelly, confident voice stopped Harold.

"...the old gods, or the new?"

Harold stared at her for a moment, jaw completely slack. He released me, assuming correctly that I'd now follow without question. I could only scamper so fast in my heels on the uneven pavement, and by the time I'd managed to jump into the SUV and slam shut the passenger's side door, he turned the key back and forth repeatedly in the ignition. But the engine didn't ignite. It didn't even rev. It just clicked like a cheap knob lock. The headlights and hazards had died too, and the car, for some reason beyond comprehension, was drained of its power.

I looked back for the woman. She couldn't be seen through the windshield—because she stood outside my window, staring. I shrieked in her too-close pale blue eyes, less than a foot from my face.

She lifted her wrinkled hand and I thought she meant to punch through the glass. I kept shouting hoarse cries as she proceeded to make a cranking gesture. Somehow, through the fog of my hysteria, I understood she was telling me *to roll down my window*.

Meanwhile, Harold composed himself and exited the car. Perhaps he remembered that he was, after all, a gargantuan, wealthy man, and had little to fear from this witchy-looking street woman. "Lady, I'm going to insist that you leave me and my colleague alone," he barked.

But she barely turned, and those wide-open eyes lasered into my own with a maddening urgency impossible to ignore. "Which is it?" she spoke again, voice dreamy and unconcerned with anything else in the world. "The old, or the n—"

Harold grabbed her and pulled her away in a drastic gesture. I panicked. Did he plan to beat her to death in a drunken rage? My thoughts tumbled. My lungs struggled to get enough air. What occurred next exploded my worldview and threatened to rip apart the Velcro of my sanity—

—for all around, the street saturated with unnatural shadows: blacker, opaquer, they wriggled at the edges like a great blanket of darkness pulled by a multitude of worms. As this scene unfolded, the being-watched feeling intensified. The old woman continued staring, yes, but my skin crawled, as I also received the impression of a thousand spying eyes trained upon my every move. The shadows themselves acted independent from any light, and they poured forward like sentient liquid, filling the cracks in the pavement and advancing over bits of scattered stone.

Not for a moment did I believe they moved without intention. They surrounded Harold from all directions, gathering around his brown oxfords. Then they crawled onto his feet. My panicked screams filled the car as I beheld the dark vines winding up and up his pant legs, up and up over his shirt, jacket, and loosely knotted tie. They crept up his neck, and his throat, over his chin, covered his cheeks, and forced themselves into his mouth, smothering his anguished shouts and causing his body to uncontrollably writhe—

—and then suddenly, it was over.

The shadows vanished. The headlights blasted on. The young women resumed their singing: *friendship never e-ends*!

The old woman remained standing outside the car's door, unmoved by recent events. I crawled across to the driver's side, jumped from the car and rushed Harold, shouting if he was okay. He looked at me stupidly, lost in a daze or trance, saying nothing.

"What did you do to him?" I demanded of the woman, but she too did not answer.

Harold remained standing upright but appeared incapable of much else. Pulling him, I could get him to take some halting steps, and in that way maneuvered him back into the passenger seat (no easy task), shut him in, then ran to the driver's side. Before entering, I noticed the body of the dead man had disappeared, as if he were a beached clump of seaweed stolen back by receding tide. I looked to the woman in the street as if she might explain the body's disappearance. As if she could explain anything.

As if anybody could.

Not knowing the meaning of my words, I shouted this to her: "I worship the new!"

Then I hit the gas.

I turned left and right, speeding for some time before spotting the blessed on-ramp to I-83, which appeared to me like a lifeline from God. Harold continued to lack language as we raced out of that hellscape of a city, back to the safety and sanity and cleanliness of the suburbs.

The situation perplexed Harold's wife, Donna, and I tried chalking up his dazed condition to too much drinking. She looked dubious, writing me off as the cause, no doubt. Maybe she thought me a hussy, as well. Once I'd gone inside to call a cab, I returned outside and finally removed the sculpture from the windshield, which would need replacing. I then hosed off the front of his car and its tires. Little bits of bones and human refuse were still smashed up into the tire's ridges.

As I watched the cleansing liquid pour over the vehicle and down onto Harold's perfectly paved driveway, the evening's strange sights replayed in my mind no matter how hard I tried stopping them. There was so much—too much—to process, but for some reason, one thing stood out that had nothing to do with the witch and her shadows. It was something Harold had said, just after we'd hit the man. "It doesn't matter," he'd tried telling me. "Killing someone doesn't matter like you think it does."

Of that much, Harold may have been right.

4

KNOW YOUR ENEMIES

We'll get back to Harold in a second, but first I need you to do something, Dear Reader. Close your eyes. Now, are they really closed? Good. Next, I want you to imagine the face of your worst enemy.

All of us have one. It could be a coworker, a spouse, a neighbor. It could be the nosy clerk at the drug store who mentally takes notes of your more sensitive purchases. One time, a client claimed his worst enemy was also his best friend. "I'll go out to the ballgame with him, and offer to buy him a dog," he told me. "I put mustard and onions on it, everything's nice. Then, on my way back to the bleachers, I can't stop fantasizing about slipping razor blades into the bun."

Perhaps you're having a hard time picturing yours, and I'll tell you why. It's because you have too many. It's true, right? When I asked you, you closed your eyes and envisioned not a single individual, but a grotesque, layered conglomerate like the product of Picasso. You combined the bully from high school, the dead-weight friend, the impossible customer, the arrogant coworker, etc. I get it. After all, it's so hard to choose just one!

Eventually, you'll advance to the stage in your destructive powers where you'll kill people randomly, without discrimination, purely for the sake of recklessness and pleasure. But when you're beginning, it's important to focus on targets whose murder would help you progress in life. Most times, this will be someone in the same professional sphere as you.

Once you've got the first, then go ahead. Make a list of all your assailants. Is there a clear #1 target? If so, it may not necessarily make sense to go after them first.

For your first list, I recommend you have exactly five targets.

Like mine did.

MEET THE DIVISION HEADS

Harold didn't come to work the next day and didn't return any calls. Considering the previous night's events, this didn't surprise me, but I couldn't stop my nerves from clenching. As far as I could tell, nobody knew he'd invited me to the downtown BDC meeting. Donna might have leaked my involvement, but I doubted if anyone asked her. What could she say, anyway? I'd been present throughout the event and still couldn't wrap my head around what occurred. We'd experienced evil magic—either that or a shared hallucination.

Worse for Harold, a leadership summit was scheduled that day. Everyone showed up, including Eva, and since he'd been responsible for giving introductory remarks, she volunteered to give the KLR "state of the union" in his place. I knew the group disagreed with Harold, but their sick joy at his absence surprised me. They looked like swine preparing to feast at the trough. We sat for a minute eyeing one another until Hank Domino got the ball rolling on some chit chat:

LIST ITEM #1: Hank Domino, The Nut

"Could be an emergency visit to the doc," Hank said with a smug, superior smile. "Maybe all the Camels finally amounted to something, in his lungs."

Hank was head of our law office and earned the nickname "The Nut" not because he was crazy (which he was), but because of his obsessions with order and health. To this end, he resorted to frequent meditation sessions, during which he closed his office door and perched upon a pillow, humming to himself between two potted plants. If someone interrupted, he would fly into an impressive rage. One time, an assistant popped in her head to let him know his personal accountant was on the line. According to eyewitnesses, Hank chewed her out and fired her at the day's end.

Besides the meditation routine, Hank also avidly exercised. He had an appalling personality, but looked quite the spitting image of manhood for being in his late-40's. His once-brown hair was settling into something sleety, parted in the middle and styled like a groomed lion.

Pleased with his dark joke, he looked about the room for a follow-up, and found one from...

LIST ITEM #2: Philip Platt, The Spy

"Dudes, want to know why Harold skipped today?" exclaimed Philip. He pointed to his temple. "This right here. He's not as quick on the uptake anymore, is intimidated by our smarts."

Philip was head of KLR's Technology and Systems, a new-ish department commanding a formidable budget. At thirty-five, he still used youthful slang and despite wearing a suit, kept his blonde hair long and uncombed to add a dash of counterculture to his appearance. He constantly referred to his "early days" on the road with a musical act called "The Big Hard Ons" or "The Hard Big Ones," or something along those lines.

Like most men in tech, he believed himself mentally superior, so it made sense he mocked Harold's intelligence. Murmurs of approval met his comment. Philip checked my reaction, aware I remained the CEO's sole ally. In fact, Philip often gave me funny looks whose meaning I couldn't pinpoint, but I suspected that underneath his cool posturing, he was a garden variety sex pervert. Besides consuming what I assumed to be copious amounts of pornography on his many computers, I believed he used technology to spy on all our actions.

"Um, even if Harold felt out of the loop, he'd still show," said...

LIST ITEM #3: Laird Ott, The File-o-Phile

...in his dry tone. Laird leaned in and looked at us from above his rectangular glasses. "It's most unusual he did not at least, um, call. What's more likely is he mixed up the dates and went on vacation, yes? Where does he like to go, Cancun? Anyone check down there, with the, um, Cancun people?"

Laird's department, Operations Management, provided only imaginary value. For him and his cronies, work consisted of fabricating non-existent problems, then publicly sounding alarms about them before sinking as many hours and resources as possible into "solving" said problems, all while disrupting normal work and adding needless bureaucratic layers to even our most basic operations.

He was a man of medium height and large girth and could not be said to have any other defining characteristics. When he walked into a room, you were never entirely sure he was there. Talking to him was pointless. Perhaps he believed himself to possess a deadpan wit, but I can't remember him ever expressing a substantive opinion. The one exception would be the topic of paperwork, for which he was notorious. His department occupied an entire floor of KLR, chock full with towering filing cabinets of long-forgotten documents.

I'm not sure anyone else heard Laird speak. The moment after he did, the most formidable member of my list stood. Yes, it was...

LIST ITEM #4: Eva LeFey, The Consultant

"Gentleman!" she said like a drill sergeant. "I'll lead today's summit. You've heard rumors that at next week's shareholder meeting, we'll be announcing some big changes to the company. All of you—or, *most* of you—have brought in much of the exciting upgrades underway at KLR. But I have two surprises to share. The first is that there's a leadership shakeup coming..."

That caused astonished murmurs. "That's awesome," said Philip, "Time to usher in the next generation."

"The next CEO could be any of us," Laird probably said.

Hank kept an even keel, sipping from his oversized mug of potent herbal tea. He said, "Hmmm. Or it could be Eva herself."

Cody, who I'll describe in detail shortly, said, "You mentioned two pieces of news. Were you saving the best for last? Because that one was pretty good."

We all looked to Eva, whose put-togetherness and grace only heightened her mystique. She was on the younger end of her thirties and held herself with preternatural confidence. Her origins must have been Nordic, maybe Eastern European, tall with long-lashed eyes set far apart on her face reminiscent of a deer, and always wearing a sly smile that said *yeah, what about it?*

"Yes, Cody. Next week will also be the announcement of... The New Product."

I gasped. Everyone did. KLR sold only The Product for so long—but Harold hadn't mentioned anything about a second. Who developed it? How would it affect us? And most importantly, why were us division heads the last to hear of it? I scanned around to see the others' reactions, but they just nodded along. Irate, I stood and slammed my fists on the table. Practically leaning on my knuckles, I said, "Why *you*, Eva, informing us of this? I have half a mind to think you invented this presentation only this morning."

Now the lot of them laughed, sharing an in-joke, and I realized that this meeting was a ruse, a cover, a technicality in which they pretended to be part of a team with Harold and me. I suddenly pictured them holding secret meetings, where the real business of The Nameless Corporation's hostile takeover transpired. The other division heads knew more than me about the shakeup and the New Product, but how much?

Later, we broke for lunch. Eva walked into the many winding corridors of KLR and I followed, calling her name, but she didn't appear to hear. I needed explanations, but her long legs carried her ahead and I jogged to keep pace. I was in no mood to be ignored, so when she nearly escaped into the elevator, I surprised myself by reaching out and grabbing the sleeve of her navy executive jacket.

I should pause to add one more note about Eva: her presence was made even more puzzling by the fact that the entire tenth floor of our HQ—the top floor—was dedicated to her and off-limits for all staff. The elevator wouldn't carry anyone to the tenth floor without a special badge. As I understand it, the Nameless Corporation set up an office, and to protect it, contracted their own security staff, separate from our own obligatory guards. I'd picked Lance's brain for clues from the grapevine, but nada. Nobody knew what she did up there.

That's why I stopped her before she got on the elevator. But her stern expression threw me for a loop. "A word of advice, Jenny," she said. "You'll understand your piece of the KLR puzzle soon. Don't worry, your role will be important. But for now, be patient."

My fingers released from her coat without meaning to, and Lance's words replayed in my head: *she can do things with her mind.*

Then I stammered as she strode into the center of the elevator, turned, and looked down on me as the doors closed from either side. "...but don't be lazy. Plenty of business lays ahead."

As I returned to my office, the day's strangeness weighed on me. I sat at my desk for a minute, clenching my fists harder and harder until I realized I couldn't unclench them. Doing so required staring at my manicured fingers, emptying my thoughts, and really willing it. My heart raced and my head felt woozy. This condition was not improved one bit by the arrival of...

LIST ITEM #5: Cody MacMillain, The Man-Child

...who entered my office wielding a football made of thick foam. I wasn't paying attention though, so when he yelled

"Think fast!" I only looked up to witness said football flying towards my nose.

I had only the recourse to think a single thought: *I hate my coworkers.*

Then the ball ricocheted off my forehead with a stinging *thwap*, and it bounced around the floor in random directions. "Gee, sorry Jenny!" he exclaimed. "Thought you saw me."

Cody jogged into my office—uninvited—and I greeted him with the most fearsome scowl I could muster. His apology's tone contained no sincerity or respect, and the only way I could calm myself as he grabbed his ball was to imagine plucking one of my fountain pens from my upright pen case and jamming it into his eye. How satisfying and relaxing it would be, watching him scream, watching the blood run down his cheek and staining his starched, white button-up.

He had the mental prowess of a golden retriever. His entire persona—from his weekend plans to all his talk of *teamwork* and *level playing fields* was rooted entirely in sports. Baseball obsessed him, and he lamented the loss of Baltimore's football team, which had been sold to Indianapolis at some point. Without sports, this man would be a man-shaped skin balloon, void inside.

"Say, Jenny, since I'm here," he started. He had the nerve to toss the ball up and down as he addressed me. "My team informs me your reimbursement requests are missing a lot of receipts. We can't just take your word for things and cut you checks, you know."

That really triggered me and I lost my cool. "Keeping track of receipts is your division's work, not mine!" I snapped. "Do I look like an accountant? I do important things, Cody. And the previous Finance Chief trusted me enough to reimburse me all the time."

"Those were the old days," he chided. "Move over and make way for the new."

Who do you worship? The old woman's creaky voice blasted in my mind in vivid surround-sound. *The old gods, or the new?*

Cody sauntered to the office door, pleased with how his comment shut me down. He then shot me two finger guns, and I pined for two guns of my own. In business—as well as witchcraft—there is always much talk of old vs. new. Everything changes, it's true. But the need for vengeance is constant.

Things weren't over between us. Not yet.

Recognize When the Pieces Come Together

A lot of clients tell me when it comes to their first killing, fears and worries parade their mind and they struggle to finish the job. This is why I urge people—and this goes for anyone, doing anything at any time—to do more and think less. There's a time and a place for thinking, but it's not at work.

Dear Reader, is there any task in your life that you put off, simply because you overthink it? I assure you, the reason you delay is not because you haven't thought *enough*. It's because you've thought too much, to the point that your conception of what to do has become monstrously overcomplicated.

Success cannot be planned. It is seized by those of us who live open and free, and who are prepared to strike with action within the fleeting, golden moments when the stars align and winning conditions arise. Most of the things people do aren't particularly inspiring, to put it lightly. But the more you accomplish, the greater your chances of achieving a breakthrough. So...

Remodeling your kitchen? *Do it.*

Calling back the IRS? *Do it.*

Pursuing your coworker down the hallway? *Do it.*

At a leisurely pace, Cody walked the many winding corridors of KLR. Whenever he stopped to lean into someone's office to chitchat, I'd duck around a corner or slip behind a plant to avoid being spotted. In this way, I pursued him to the breakroom in the northeast corner of the sixth floor. Its features include a decent kitchenette, a seating area with several tables, and windows providing an exceptional view of the back parking lot.

Through a crack in the door, I spied Cody. He retrieved his lunch bag from the fridge and put something in the toaster. I assumed he'd take a seat, but he instead headed to the sink and started filling it with steamy water. A minute later, he started doing dishes. I rolled my eyes. Of course Cody would use his break to do others' dishes. It was an easy way to score brownie points later.

I had no plan. No worrisome doubts crowded my skull. Right then, I lived fully and vehemently in the moment. Had I fretted over x, y and z things that might go wrong, I'd have psyched myself out and returned to the seminar.

The blood in my veins ran cold like a lizard, and I padded through the kitchen, approaching, while the hissing faucet masked the steps of my heels. Counter space was tight, and the toaster oven lived direcctly next to the sink. Through its clear glass front, the heating coils glowed intense as magma.

Out of everything terrible in the last twenty-four hours, this man-child hitting me with his football represented the worst of it. Dear Reader: chalk it up to exhaustion, or my recent brush with death, or perhaps an undiagnosed chemical imbalance, but whatever the reason, I craved seeing his motionless body. I wanted him dead. He deserved it. And I wasn't about to overthink my way out executing the grim task at hand.

It's funny, but Cody looked at me and smiled in the last seconds of his life. I reached past him, grabbed the toaster and pushed it into the sink, but the act failed to register as anything dangerous. He had probably already forgotten hitting me, and looked perfectly satisfied and in charge of his circumstances. Sometimes I wonder, *what were his last words about to be?* Probably, *Oh, hi Jenny.*

God, what a jerk.

From the outside, the effect of the volts surging through his body appeared subtle. His eyes rolled toward the ceiling and his mouth quivered as if aroused. Though the sink fizzed and sparked, no screaming occurred, just a breathless *hk-hk-hk*, and his body juddered, remaining upright on both feet. I wanted to ask him if being electrocuted felt good, but by the time the question occurred, he'd died.

His knees slumped to the floor, dragging his body down with them. He didn't fall all the way and instead crumpled into a supplicant's pose, drooling face smooshed sideways against the cabinet. I poked him a couple times to see if he'd jolt back to life, then checked for a pulse on his throat's still-warm skin. This only confirmed that Cody would not be attending any big games this coming weekend, or ever again.

I stared, awed and elated, until struck by the fear of being caught. I tiptoed to the kitchen door and peeked out my head: left, right, the hallway was empty in both directions. We'd been alone the entire time.

Someone had made coffee earlier and I grabbed a cup, stirring in two hazelnut creamers. I then headed back to the conference room. Considering what I'd just accomplished, I think I held my composure rather well: my hands were steady, I shed no tears of remorse or delight. By the time I'd taken my seat near the head of the table, someone may have stumbled upon Cody's corpse back in the kitchen, but nobody at the meeting questioned his absence. Nobody asked after him, and word of his death hadn't traveled upstairs to the leadership summit, yet.

I sat among the surviving division heads with my secret, feeling much more capable of tackling the afternoon's agenda. A minute later, Eva returned from the tenth floor and said, "Hope you all had a productive lunch break," and I couldn't help but wonder if she directed her statement, in particular, at me.

5

FIND A MENTOR

I'd just committed my first murder and felt great Friday and Saturday night. But the greatness came crashing down by Sunday morning, as I lay in my bed staring up at crystalline light fixture hanging from the ceiling. I wished I had some guidance, someone with whom I could talk things through, but murder invites too much stigma and controversy. I tried calling Harold but Donna answered. She told me he wasn't speaking, and they considered taking him in for a stay at Sheppard Pratt hospital. By killing my enemy, The Emptiness ended up bigger than ever. Something about the way I did it felt wrong, or not good enough.

After your first kill, Dear Reader, I recommend you set aside some time to reflect and jot some notes on the following:

1. **Was your victim all the way dead, or did they survive?**

2. **Did killing them fulfill you emotionally—or was something missing?**

3. For next time, what steps can you take to improve your performance?

By the time Monday morning rolled around, I realized Cody had got off easy. It was a transactional murder, one that simply ended his life. He'd felt no fear, and I delivered no message. His body was discovered by Wendy Slatsky in Accounts Payable—which I imagine dampened her lunch hour—and the paramedics chalked up the death to accident, which I found hilarious but also a little underwhelming. Nobody suspected me.

And I wasn't sure how I felt about that.

Shouldn't they? How else was I to be respected, to be feared?

Before driving to work, I searched the house for inspiration: a paring knife, a mallet, and an ax John never used all presented themselves. Sure, they'd do the trick, and their use could not be construed as accidents, but were too pedestrian, too domestic. Somehow, the idea of using a gun seemed even more banal. After all, guns are what every American uses to solve their problems.

I needed something special. Something otherworldly. And for the rest of my regularly scheduled Monday, I daydreamed nonstop about the woman on the abandoned street in downtown Baltimore. Who was she, and what magic did she wield? I witnessed her curse Harold for his behavior, which terrified me, but still felt kinship. Perhaps if I returned and tried to reason with her, I could get her to lift Harold's curse. And perhaps she could go into further detail about her occult powers.

What she did to Harold? That was my kind of energy.

That night, after dinner at Red Lobster with Catherine, I jumped into my van and headed downtown in search of a street sorceress. I knew we'd been in the East part of the city around North Avenue, but in my panic hadn't noted any relevant landmarks. None stood out either, for the blocks in the area look similar with their rows of tightly packed rowhomes. I searched for over an hour, an experience that challenged my notions of America. The streets showed me abandoned corners outside my conception of a civil, just and profitable country. No wonder my parents fled.

Eventually I spotted a clue: a long stone wall with imposing barb wire installed on top. It turned out to surround a massive cemetery spanning at least six square blocks. The woman's house was somewhere along one of its walls, I remembered, and I located the right street by driving the graveyard's perimeter. Recalling the exact house proved tricky, but a group of men in oversized white t-shirts hanging out on a stoop might help. Steeling my nerves, I pulled over to talk to them, and to my surprise one jogged over so I rolled down my window.

He looked young, wore a thin platinum chain and had a shaved head. He said, "Gold Star twenty a cap. In the Hole forty."

"Oh, for drugs?" I blurted in response. "What kind? How will they make me feel?"

I genuinely wanted to know, but it seemed salesmanship wasn't in his wheelhouse. He walked back toward his group, shaking his head. I grabbed my purse and exited, following, making sure my heels didn't catch in the cracked pavement.

"Um, excuse me? I might be interested in drugs," I called. Something about my presence caught everyone off guard, and their conversation cut out the next instant. There were four men, and they all looked at me curiously before standing upright and approaching, forming a semi-circle.

"Homegirl looks like my fifth-grade teacher," said one.

"Ha, right. That's good," I said. "But I came down here looking for something..."

"Girl, what those kids do to you?" exclaimed another.

All of them laughed. All but one. He was skinnier than the others and walked up very close to my face. "What that bag made of, teacher? My girl lost a bag like this. Same bag." Without grabbing it, he placed his hands around it, never looking away.

For my part, I didn't look away either, and I swung my bag over my shoulder and out of his reach. "First of all, I'm not a teacher. Do I look that pathetic? And second, this purse is mine. I bought it at Michael Kors. And third, I didn't come here for drugs, though I might have bought a bunch if that guy answered my question. Anyway, I didn't come here to talk to you all either. I came here looking for an old woman."

"That's what I'm lookin' at right now."

"Different old woman. Older than me. And I think she's a witch."

"Boys," spoke a voice behind them, and everyone stopped. "You know who she seeks. No need to give her a hard time. Not yet, at least."

Keeping their eyes on me, the men stepped aside to reveal the woman who'd accosted Harold and me last Thursday. She was dressed in what I remembered was the same multicolored shawl and headpiece. Her outfit evoked a certain regalness, though overworn and tattered. She asked, "So what brings you back to my neighborhood, Miss Lady?"

I smoothed down the rumples in my suit and took two steps forward, clearing the ring of men, then extended her a handshake. "My name is Jenny Johnston, and I'm VP of

Product Services at KLR, Inc. My CEO and I experienced an accident here the other day, but I wanted to discuss..." I stopped, sensing her attention waning. This line of negotiation wouldn't budge this woman, so I took a deep breath and readjusted. "First, do you know what happened to the man?"

The old woman shook her head, slowly.

"Right, well, I'm very sorry about that and I've alerted the police," I continued, eliciting a laugh from the small crowd. "But the real reason I came back is to speak with you. I saw you summon the shadows and do something to Harold...that's my CEO. Can what you did to him...be undone? He's been unable to speak or do anything constructive all week."

She gestured for me to follow, and we walked up a cracked stoop into a house. The men returned to their own stoop and resumed their business as if none of this had happened. I had to wait for the woman to walk up the stoop, which she did carefully, with slow steps. No doorknob or key was needed to open her front door, she simply pushed and it creaked inward. Then we entered the run-down house.

The room beyond looked to my eyes like more of a cabin than a home. Much was in disrepair—a huge piece of the ceiling had caved in, and at some point in history a maniac must have attacked random spots on the walls with a sledgehammer. On the floor sat a television with a bent rabbit ear antenna. Indiscernible images played across its blue, fuzzy screen. Hung high above were the many heads of taxidermized animals: a deer, a groundhog, a fox, as well as collections of squirrels and rats, all staring through the mote-filled air from unblinking eyes.

"My name is Denise," she said. "Much is possible, Miss Jenny. Anything you can imagine, in fact, can be done. But by the will of the old gods, what is done cannot be undone.

Do you understand?"

"I think so."

"But that's not why you drove down here, is it?"

Everything smelled like a wet blanket. There was a fireplace looking long unused, above it a portrait of someone singing passionately. At least I assumed they were singing, because their head was thrust backward with mouth wide open. I shook my head at her question.

Until then, Denise didn't look at me directly, but more around me in my general direction. Here she fixed her stare upon me and squinted, as if peering through my skin. "What did they do to you?" she whispered. "What did they do to make you hurt so bad?"

My eyes got hot and bleary and I grabbed a packet of tissues from my purse. "They...they don't give me the respect that I deserve."

"You deserve a lot of respect, Jenny?"

I nodded. "Before making VP, I was top seller in my division for two years. And now I'm by far the most productive of my team, but the other division heads and the consultant pretend like I'm an enemy."

"...and what are you, Jenny?"

"A boss," I said. "I ought to be everyone's boss."

"Even of the guy you were with?"

I shook my head. My perfect plan from last week now seemed like a distant, lunatic dream that would never actualize. I thought Harold and I could be partners, but what I hadn't admitted—even to myself—was that I just saw him as an opportunity to climb higher. In an ideal world, I'd be above him. But now I was a nobody, with nothing under my belt but a measly murder.

"Listen," I said. "You're right. I'm not super interested in you undoing your curse on Harold. I need something from you. I want to be able to do what you do."

"No, no. Nobody wants to do what I do."

"That isn't true. If I had your powers, I could do terrible things to—"

"Miss Jenny," Denise cut me off. "I am revered as a great priestess in Baltimore. Those men outside, they are my acolytes. And now you stand inside my temple. It's possible for me to grant you the powers of the old gods, but why should I? You have nothing to give to me in return."

"What about money?"

"Look around you. You think I'm interested in money?"

I walked away, dejected. Outside, the men waved goodbye, one even shouting that he only joked earlier. The sun was just setting, and the shadows collecting along the sidewalk compelled me to hurry.

I sat in my car and cried for a minute, thinking about the mess my life had become, driving into the heart of this wretched city in search of magic I didn't understand. I turned the ignition and idled another minute, hand gripping the shift lever and foot tapping the clutch, but couldn't bring myself to drive. Not yet. I couldn't let Denise chase me off that easy. She had something that I wanted her to sell me. This meant that I was a customer. And I always tell my clients, when it comes to negotiation...

Always Embrace the Customer Mindset

One day when I was eighteen, I learned a valuable lesson: it's not what's right, it's *who's* right. This transpired at a county boutique, where I wanted to purchase a pair of fashionable bell bottoms. They were pretty, deep blue denim with embroidered pockets. Only one pair was left in my size, and I snatched it off the rack and carried it to the counter, pleased with myself and eager to impress whoever looked at me.

The clerk also looked to be about my age and size, and when I handed them to her, she pouted. "These aren't for sale," she said, stuffing them into some drawer on her side. I couldn't believe it, but knew she wanted them for herself.

"I found them, I want to buy them, they're mine!" I spat from across the counter, but she only rolled her eyes. I wasn't yet of an age to speak to the manager, and I turned before spinning back once more and staring her down.

She remained unmoved. "Really want 'em so bad?" she asked. "Price went up. Fifty dollars."

I hadn't planned on spending more than ten. Outraged, I slammed down my open palm and walked back to my car. Then I spotted something in the car parked next to mine: a wallet resting on the passenger side seat. The door was locked, so I smashed a brick through the window and snatched it up. Lady luck blessed me—it contained over sixty bucks. I marched back in and purchased the jeans.

Of course, it wasn't over between me and the shifty shop keep. I pulled into a shadowy corner of a building across the street and waited two hours for her to close. The cops came and went to investigate the auto theft, but nobody saw me, waiting. When the clerk finally drove away, I followed at a distance until she pulled up to her house. Noting the location, I went to the store and bought a beef heart, then returned after dark to leave a messy present on her windshield.

The point is, if you feel in charge, there's always a way.

Back in my van, I recalled that triumphant customer service interaction as I searched around for inspiration, but only found empty coffee cups and a pair of sunglasses. Money didn't interest Denise, but surely, I had something I could trade for her services. What about the crummy van itself? I didn't see any vehicles nearby, maybe she needed one. I pondered the thought briefly while continuing to look around, then I opened my glovebox and saw my best chance.

A catalogue for The Product.

I snatched it out and marched back up the stoop into Denise's modest residence. Arms crossed, she emerged from another room and eyed me warily until I showed her. She reluctantly took it and I watched her demeanor transform to curiosity as she thumbed through the pages. "What is this, Miss Jenny?"

Ah, The Product. KLR's defining asset. In my darkest hours, I always returned to my love for it. It comes in so many varieties, shapes, and even different colors. Different sizes, potencies. In and of itself, it has no value. And yet it inspires pure wantonness in all who see it.

"Even with all my powers, this I can't produce," Denise said. "The Old Gods cannot create it."

And I knew I held in my hands the power of the New.

"I can get this to you," I promised. "Anything you see from those pages can be yours." Technically that was a lie, as complicated processes for delivering The Product existed and supply remained in such demand that even paying clients still awaited their deliveries. Then of course there was its prohibitively expensive price. But I'd deal with the red tape later.

She leaned out her front door and summoned her associates. They conferred in the doorway, speaking in hushed tones and flipping through the catalog. She returned to me and pointed out several items, and demanded the quantity she'd need, and I nodded.

"I can gift you my powers through a ritual," Denise said after we shook on the deal. "But it requires responsibility and sacrifice. The great N'Thydolarp, It That Devours Sanity, will visit after you use the power. It will require payment and will collect, and collect, and collect, for all the rest of your days. Let me ask you, Jenny. You are so close to the New Gods. They are at your fingertips. Are you certain you wish to resort to the powers of the Old?"

"Were I not certain, I wouldn't be here," I said. "When it comes to my coworkers, it's not just about their death. It's about style."

My response suited Denise just fine. She led me down a shadowy hall. On the way, I spied a hole blasted into the floor that revealed an ominous darkness. We passed through what once must have been a kitchen, full of rusted and long unused appliances. Then we exited the back door and emerged into a weed-choked backyard lined with a weathered wood fence. The buzzing of bees surrounded us and what looked like an amateur apiary occupied the yard's far side.

Denise instructed me to envision my enemies. One after the other, I forced a slideshow of their leering faces into my mind's eye: Philip, Hank, Laird, Eva, and the recently departed Cody. Denise next instructed me to picture my place of work, and my home, and I did that too, seeing the KLR headquarters and then picturing my commute between it and Valley Fields.

She placed her pruney fingers on my face and whispered in a language I didn't recognize. Even though I did not understand the meaning, her words produced a physical effect. They wriggled into my ears and crisscrossed my brain, forming a latticework that covered my mind. Calm isn't the right word for how this made me feel; it was more sedated. She withdrew and bent down to open a cupboard-like piece of furniture nestled among so many eccentric potted plants and unlabeled glass bottles. From it, she took out a skull which might once have belonged to a goat.

"Hold," she commanded. I took it into my hands and noticed it was fitted with leather and cloth straps, and covered in revolting brown stains whose origins would soon become clear. Denise left and quickly returned with a bottle of dark red syrup which she uncorked, and she poured from it into a hole at the skull's apex.

The backyard became warmer. My deodorant and perfume did their best to mask the stink rising from my armpits, though I didn't know how my face fared as I sweated profusely. I quaked beneath my skin. I questioned my actions. Perhaps my quest for carnage had already finished and I had, without purpose, driven myself beyond all reason into the realm of irreversible madness.

Denise continued speaking in tongues, words warping my mind further. My vision blurred and my ability to orient my body in time and space waned. Which direction was the dirt and which the sky seemed inconsequential, as I suddenly felt more in tune with the impossibly vast universe. In this discombobulated state, I lost any sense of identity and became something like a puppet. My limbs loosened and limbered and swayed as if I danced a samba, all the while gripping my blood-filled vessel of bone. Beyond it, I perceived only a crimson-flecked darkness, shot through with passing bees, and within that sunless void I made out two giant, luminous eyes.

My movements subsided and my hands lifted the skull so that it sat even with my face. As Denise intoned, the surrounding dark spun at a gentle, even keel, but I felt very rooted and solid. Hands and fingers acting of their own accord, I lifted the skull and unplugged a cork inserted into its snout. I then extended my tongue and let the liquid pour freely, trickling into my waiting mouth. It tasted vile yet sweet, like the drippings that might collect beneath composting cherries, cut with rotten steak and infused with tin. I gagged and gargled and cackled, and some spilled over my cheek and down my neckline in rivulets.

The liquid infected me with power. If previously untethered to reality, I now inhabited an entirely different dimension. I sailed down a tunnel of fantastic colors and otherworldly beings taunted me. I saw something like a black shark with angel's wings, and a hybrid monster with horse legs, a man's torso, and a blocky computer monitor for a head. Cries and wails and the music of the damned echoed everywhere. I reached out to a nearby spectator and my hand appeared far away, elsewhere, yet somehow still connected to my body.

I knew not how long I existed in such a state, but after some time returned to the world of Baltimore: to the backyard of Denise's rowhome on the shadowy city street, and to my corporeal self, feeling for the first time reborn.

"There she is," said Denise. There were others present nearby, and they murmured with approval as I glanced about the humid darkness. When I stood from the patch of dirt where I'd apparently collapsed, I looked around changed. I was a different woman.

Denise and the bystanders clapped. Somebody handed me a glass of water. Sipping it, I tasted pure liquid imagination.

"Now go home," Denise told me.

And so I did.

•

My return drive was one of the most wondrous experiences of my life. The highway that extended before me was a great, glittering ribbon, and the sky above swirled like Van Gogh. I felt hope and possibility, unassailed by any nagging inner monologue. No worries over money, appearance, or my housekeeping staff. All of that melted away.

Only one challenge remained, as it remains for you, Dear Reader. As I visualized it with unwavering clarity and purpose, I pressed the gas harder, going one hundred, one-ten, one-twenty up the highway. The remaining challenge, of course, was work.

As I entered the area of my town, strange events occurred all around. I sped towards a yellow light but didn't make it before it turned red. Yet in the blink of an eye, the same light became green yet again. I thought I'd simply imagined that, but then, in a move most unusual, two cars and a milk truck in front of me all simultaneously pulled over to the shoulder without my needing to honk or flick my high beams like usual.

Those were mere oddities, however, compared to when I got home. I stepped out of the van and stared across the street. By then, the sky was the royal blue of dawn, and the streetlamps were still on, and I saw clearly the hideous beige paint job on the Myers' home. How it taunted me! How I wished that shade would melt into the ether and become replaced by the respectable white of yore.

And then, Dear Reader: it did.

It did exactly that. The house turned white.

And from all the way in the Kiesling's backyard, the braying of Mr. King assaulted my ears. I cringed and shut my eyes, only to discover that by doing so, I now saw the dog quite clearly, as if a film played in my mind. Only it wasn't a film. Nor was it my imagination. I actually projected my sight and surveyed their back yard, from afar.

Standing in my driveway with my eyes closed, I watched Mr. King in this way, running in circles and peeking through the slats in their fence. And through sheer will of mind, I reached—without hands, and without moving—across my own yard and into the Kiesling's, and I reached into the beagle's throat, and I stole away its voice with invisible fingers.

The dog paced, confused, as it attempted to whine and bark without effect. It opened its mouth and tried to bellow, but all that could be heard were its smacking lips and its anxious paws padding back and forth across the grass. Though it was early, the young Brad Kiesling, no older than ten, slid open the glass back door and approached the dog. I heard as the boy asked, "Everything okay, King?"

I decided I didn't want to steal the dog's voice. No, that wasn't enough.

As I reached back into the dog, the boy knelt and scratched his beloved beagle underneath its chin. "Is everything okay?" he asked again.

Mr. King's meaty tongue sucked back into its mouth, and it sat very upright. Perhaps the boy noticed a subtle change in the dog's demeanor, how a hard coldness entered its black, glassy eyes. Surely, the boy was caught off guard when these same eyes turned to regard him in a very human way. The dog then replied, using the weary voice of an old man: "My life is a lie. You keep me as a prisoner. For God's sake, you little brat, have mercy on my canine soul and put me down!"

Now it was the boy our neighborhood heard.

I walked back into my house to get a couple hours of sleep. I needed to rest, I knew, for today would be huge, and I could not wait to get back to work.

PART 2

6

PAPERCUTS

Seated with one leg over the other and arms crossed, Laird Ott looked uncomfortable. Stacks of paper surrounded him: piling in trays, arranged in haphazard piles across his desk, and even edging out from atop the many filing cabinets crowding his seventh-floor office. The papers didn't bother him, though. Supposedly, he thrived in chaos. Though he understood little of how to decorate or maintain a workspace in any aesthetically pleasing sense, he still put much thought into the area's appearance. Such disarray had been designed to give an impression of constant busyness to any passer-by. Of course, nothing could be further from the truth. Laird's entire department barely did anything, and everyone at KLR knew it.

Perhaps that was what bothered him. Who can know for sure? Either way, he decided to stand and walk to his office doorway and lean through it.

"Uh, Patti?" he said to his assistant, who sat at her own tidy desk filling out check requests. Before he'd said her name, she looked relatively comfortable, but now sat bolt upright and alert. Laird speaking at all, on any topic, could very well portend a bad afternoon. She'd know this better than anyone.

Slowly, she turned to face her boss. "What is it, Laird?"

While his eyes remained unemotional and quasi-predatory, he crossed his arms again, tightly, and made that weird half smile/half frown one makes when they smush together their upper and lower lips. "Say, um, I have an idea. From now on, why don't you call me Mr. Ott? Don't you think that sounds nicer, more professional?"

She couldn't help but cringe. The way he said it, like the way he said most things to her and everyone else (but particularly to her), walked a tightrope between uncertain jest and utter seriousness. It was a joke with a taunting, domineering edge, delivered with a weaselly lack of confidence. No doubt masking deep contempt, Patti tried reorienting in a semi-productive direction. "Can I help you?"

"Hm? Can you...*help* me? Why yes, I suppose you may be able to. Ha ha, we'll see. To begin, Patti, sometimes I, um—I feel you and I struggle to communicate, and I wonder why that is."

He dragged over a nearby rolling chair and sat. Patti took a deep breath and set down the pen she'd been using, and for some reason, Laird reached across her and picked it up, and he smiled at it as if privately amused. "You see," he started, "Last week, I took the time—quite a lot of time, in fact—to explain that whenever we receive a TPS report from another department, we need to make two copies of the cover sheet, not one. The first is to be filed along with the report, and the second—"

"—is to be stored in the cover sheet filing system. I know, Laird."

Now his voice raised in register and tone, bordering on the girlish. "Do you know? Because when I checked earlier this morning, I noticed none of the cover sheets from the previous week had been filed in the—"

"I'm working on it." She gestured around the main office in which she sat, full of trays and inboxes, which themselves were crammed full of information request forms. "But ever since you added these extra regulations to our filing system, everything takes twice as long."

He muttered, "If you aren't capable of doing your job—"

Patti stood up suddenly, while he remained seated. "Now, Laird, I'm perfectly capable of doing my job!" she said. "The only thing holding me back is you. And if you care about the filing system so much, why don't you help for once instead of complaining and micromanaging everything?"

That shocked him. Perhaps Patti had never spoken up for herself like that before. Perhaps nobody had, to him. Lacking the ability to respond, his eyes darted to the floor and he rapped his knuckles twice on her desk, hard enough that the leaves of her potted plant bristled. "Um, uh, good talk, Patti. Good talk. We'll circle back to this next week once you've had some time to, um, review."

He wheeled his chair away from her, stood, and took a single step before she murmured, "You're a *sucky* boss."

That stopped him in his tracks. He took a breath in an effort to compose himself, but nonetheless wheeled back around in her direction. "Uh, uh, um. Ha ha, did you have something else you wanted to add?"

Though there was a single tear in her eye, she wiped it off and didn't stutter as she raised her voice and said out loud, again: "You're not a good, boss, Laird. Nobody thinks so. You're an asshole."

Heat crept into his face and he raised his voice to match hers. On the off chance any of the division's other employees eavesdropped, Laird wouldn't want to be heard not cutting back at her. "Sorry if I hurt your feelings by giving you feedback, but that's my specialty. And it's why they pay me the big bucks. Managing you people is, um, taking years off my life, know that? It's two cover sheets. Got it? Not one, *two*. And if you can't figure that out, maybe you can figure out how to buy yourself a pair of high heels, instead of those tennis shoes. Did you ever think about me, how when I introduce you to a client, they see, uh, uh, those disgusting loafers?"

He laughed, not waiting for a response and not manly enough to witness her reaction. He stormed out of his suite and down the hall, in the direction of someone else to bother. When he got out to the main section of his floor, he found it unusually empty. The cubicles were cleared out. No little groups chatted about Must See TV near the water cooler. The copier was unattended and dormant, and no clicking of keystrokes or warbling desk phones were heard.

The quiet must have struck him as unusual. Nonetheless, he sat at the front desk and sorted through files. This, apparently, was what he did to relax when he thought nobody was there to watch him. Of course, someone was watching him—closely. It was me.

And I turned the corner of the office to greet him.

"Hiya, Laird."

He startled, not having heard me striding with my unusually light step. He looked up, then away, in his dismissive style, before glancing back up. Perhaps he noticed some new twinkle in my eye or my relaxed, confident demeanor. "I'm afraid I have some bad news, Laird-buddy."

"Oh yeah? What's that?"

"I need to request some data from your department."

The word *data* put him at ease, and he looked a little overeager. "Ah-ha, I see. That's a very big ask, but I'm here to help." He spun around and walked in his rolling chair toward the steel cabinets across the aisle. Wandering this entire floor, you'd see these cabinets everywhere, stacked to the ceiling and full of paperwork whose purpose could not possibly have been comprehended, even by the record-keepers. The so-called procedures for storing these files occupied so much time and mental real estate that his employees were alienated from the meaning of their work. From one of these jam-packed cabinets, he produced a pile of complicated forms, which he placed on the desk before me.

"What I'll need, ah, from you," he informed me. "Is to fill out—"

"Oh, I already did that."

It made sense that my suddenly holding a huge, unwieldy stack of paper surprised Laird; I hadn't been moments before. "Riiight," he said, disbelieving that a birdbrain like myself could ever fill out the tiny boxes and fields on the myriad sheets that defined his existence. He grabbed my papers, licked a finger, then started to inspect them for mistakes, one after the other, and I beheld as his cynicism transformed to curiosity, then to something adjacent to awe. "*You*...did all this *work*, Jenny? You, uh, even managed to fill out form B-35x properly. Even my own staff struggles with that one."

"Of course they do. It's unclear whether the field is redundant to field C-64."

He smacked his lips and swallowed as if suddenly dehydrated.

I said, "So I just went ahead and filled out both sets accurately and recommended a clarification."

Incredulous, he flipped through the sheets in search of the offending field. But his fingers moved haphazardly, a little too hasty, and one of the sheets made a razor thin cut in the uppermost skin crease in his pointer finger. He cursed at the ensuing tiny frown that puckered open in his flesh. It was deep, and from the way he winced appeared quite painful. Out of that injury emerged a bead of crimson that popped into a trickle.

Composing himself, Laird stuffed the finger into his mouth like a little boy, or a vampire. He then utilized a nearby Kleenex as makeshift gauze. He navigated his rolling chair to another desk and opened one of its drawers with his uninjured hand. From that drawer he produced a new sizable stack of forms. "Thank you for taking the time to, uh, properly fill out the papework, Jenn—"

"It took no time at all."

"—uh, right. Anyway, just this week, er—just today in fact—my department saw fit to institute *new* requirements that clarify any data requests. The bad news, one might say, is that there's additional paperwork. A lot, actually. The good news, however, is that my team will have a better—clearer—understanding of your needs, and all of us here at KLR will work towards a mutual understanding of how data plays a function in all our roles."

Dear Reader: I did not slouch. I did not sigh. The smile on my face remained frozen like Mona Lisa's. I extended my hands, gestured with my fingers. "No problem, Laird," I intoned. "Hand 'em my way, big boy."

Literally anyone else, including me, would have reamed him out right then and there, which is why my utter nonchalance unnerved him. When he placed the papers in my hands, I felt him relax at having diverted me—if only briefly—from forcing him to do anything helpful. Second stack in hand, I turned one hundred and eighty degrees on my heels. Then I closed my eyes and, using my omniscient vision, observed as Laird leaned back, assuming the day's battle won.

So I opened my eyes and turned once more, completing a circle.

And I placed the papers before him. "All finished," I said. "Easy peasy, lemon squeezy."

He sat upright and his smile vanished. Now my turn for mirth had arrived. He grabbed the forms in a frenzy, and his breathing turned ragged and doglike as he flipped through them. "N-no. This is impossible. I just gave these to you. Did you, uh, uh...sneak in here beforehand and fill these all out, Jenny—did you?" He didn't look up for my response, probably didn't want it. The forms consumed his entire vision. One sheet after the other with checked checkboxes, fields full of accurate number strings and data tallied through page-length tables, all hand-printed in attractive and flawlessly legible handwriting. His lack of composure resulted in a second nasty paper cut—deeper, longer—and this time he cried in pain.

"Jenny, how are you doing this?" he shouted, fresh cut oozing red.

Perhaps he deserved a response, but if I'd supplied it, would he really understand? Either way, by the time he looked up, I'd disappeared, and he was once more the solitary occupant of the vast seventh floor.

•

BUILD YOUR COSTUME

And where did I go? Why, I strutted through the lobby toward KLR's carousel-style entrance/exit. As high noon with its scarce shade approached, I slipped on my sunglasses. I marched through the baking parking lot, hopped in the van, then piloted it through traffic at reckless speeds, weaving down York Road to my favorite destination: The Towson Town Mall.

The Mall is where I go to clear my mind. To refresh myself, to rejuvenate, and, in the case of that day, to entirely reinvent my image. What better symbol of hope and commercial transformation exists in America than the mall? A sanitized, air-conditioned marketplace where consumers of all ages and most races and some creeds max out their credit cards to become more closely aligned in appearance to the ideal images they've painted of themselves in their minds.

Many of my favorite memories transpired at the mall. When Catherine was little, we'd go after school. If she got an A on a test or report card, I'd take her to Kay-Bee Toys, and she'd pick out whichever Barbie she wanted. She loved it, but I treasure those experiences more than she did any doll.

That day, I first visited the luminous Hecht's department store, where I selected a pair of square-toed, lace-up Ralph Lauren high heels. I then strolled into the mall proper and stopped in the Banana Republic, purchasing a wide-shouldered woman's two-piece that cost a pretty penny. I strutted from that store in my new garments, each black as a raven's eye.

But my brownish blonde hair with its boring bangs presented a problem, so I marched up to Sally's Stylez on the top floor. I had no appointment, but as luck would have it, a spot opened the exact moment I set foot within the establishment. The hairdresser ushered me into one of the hydraulic styling chairs, then listened dutifully to my request. "That's quite the big change!" exclaimed my platinum-blonde stylist as she chewed her pungent Bubblicious. "No streaks, no highlights? You sure you want it all the way?"

"Just as I said," I repeated, grinning at my own reflection in the salon's oval mirror. "No variations in the color. Just the darkest black your dye can produce, and a haircut like Meg Ryan's."

WHY APPEARANCES MATTER

More than intellect, wit or moral standing, in our relationships with strangers and loved ones alike, appearances matter above all else. A tidy, attractive and considered outward appearance can elevate harlots to royalty and can curry favor with straight and homosexual men alike.

Your appearance includes physical fitness, your posture, your grooming, and most importantly, your costume. According to scientific studies undergone at Johnston Research, perfecting these elements of your outward appearance allows you to:

- **Lie more convincingly to others, as attractive people are considered 77% more trustworthy**
- **Attract the weak-willed and the simpering, who suffer from low self-esteem and frequently seek out and obey attractive leaders**
- **Make an outward show of your material wealth, as most people envy and respect those who have the time and money to attend to how they look every day**

...but it's not as simple as purchasing the most expensive and flattering clothing (although doing so is mandatory). If you are to have any value to others, you must also consider your brand.

That's right—just as chain restaurants and sneaker manufacturers and arms dealers sink significant resources into crafting their image, you too must begin building yourself up as a brand. And you must pay vigilant attention to it every time you leave the house (and most times you're inside it). If it helps, pretend a tiny video camera follows you and everyone you know, always, and it records everything you do and magically projects your image out to the world.

It's never too late to reinvent your brand. Walking through the mall that day, I appeared to its occupants a bland, woman-shaped lump of careerism. I needed to fit in with the crowd so hard I ended up looking like nothing at all. But when I exited from Sally's Stylez, and after a hasty pit stop at the Hot Topic, I emerged as a dark queen of supernatural warfare.

FUN FACT:

in 1995 alone, American companies spent 163 billion dollars in advertising!

fare. My shoes, suit, artfully tousled hair, even my lips and eyebrows—all were the dark and shiny shade of murder.

FOLLOW THE PAPER TRAIL

You may be wondering: *what's going on with Laird back at the seventh floor of KLR?* Don't worry, I'd been keeping close watch. You forget, I had developed extraordinary powers for multitasking. And today I was busy—so much remained undone!

When I sat behind the wheel of my van contemplating my new ride, I also watched as Laird stalked around his office to fulfill my request.

This eventually led him into the fabled filing complex: a massive, walled-off room (if a space so large can truly be considered a room) in which only certain of his division-members were allowed. In a small, pathetic way, it thrilled me to follow him inside. The area beyond featured no windows, and one needed to squint to see very far in the light provided by the overhead-hanging lamps. Towering filing cabinets lined long aisles that stretched every direction into cavernous darkness. So narrow were the aisles, they couldn't provide space enough for two to walk side by side. But that was no matter, for Laird was alone.

He hummed an anxious tune, and his heels clicked on the hard linoleum. Unexpectedly, a frigid gust of wind blew through, and some of the pages he carried got caught up in the draft. He must have wondered if the HVAC system had surged, and as he bent over to snatch the fallen sheets, he heard something unusual: the tiny, unmistakable creaking of one of the nearby cabinet drawers opening without any human aid.

A single piece of paper emerged from the cabinet, as if drawn forth by an invisible hand. It lingered in the stale air, then flitted with unnatural grace in his direction. The sight hypnotized him. But if he'd turned and looked around, he'd notice another cabinet drawer opening behind him, and another piece of paper becoming withdrawn. This phenomenon occurred all around, and the various sheets hovered and danced a secret choreography.

The first piece arrived above Laird's head. Though high in the air, Laird could read its single line of text, written in the center of the page in twelve-point courier font: *if you love files so much, why don't you become one?*

The floating sheet turned so that it faced diagonally downward. Then, in a straight line, it descended. It whipped around Laird's arm, fusing with the cloth of his shirtsleeve and rolling around his forearm with a vice-like grip. The piece that hovered behind Laird darted around his head just as an overdue scream emerged. To silence him, it slapped itself across his mouth and nose, sealing in his wail.

Per my specifications, his eyes remained unobstructed. The mean-spirited papers looked normal in the visual sense, yet their normality could not be verified by his tongue. It tried puncturing a hole but found the durability of this evil worksheet quite strong, with a tactile quality closer to that of rubbery skin.

More assaulted Laird, each gluing itself to his arms and legs. With terrific strength, they pulled the squirming bureaucrat down the central aisle. Oh, he tried fighting. He inaudibly cursed and gnashed. But no amount of thrashing on his part could delay my ministrations. The shackles of stationery dragged him down around a bend in the wall of cabinets, then another, and then deeper into the shadowy filing complex than he'd ever been. At the long aisle's very distant end stood a cabinet that neither Laird nor any other living being had ever witnessed before. It awaited his arrival.

THE REAL SECRET TO SUPERNATURAL TORMENT

In a minute, I'll share this secret with you, and I urge you to use it wisely. Dear Reader, I say with great seriousness that much effort is wasted on ordinary, pedestrian murder. Think back on my lackluster interaction with Cody. His death left me completely empty, for it was a mere discontinuation of his conscious experience, an uninspiring flick of the light switch, powering down his mortal meat suit.

What made all my subsequent kills and eviscerations much more effective was the application of nightmare logic.

In order to exact retribution, you must tap into the deep well of subconscious fear. Fear is formless. It is nameless. I remember how, as a five-year-old girl, a seemingly simple nightmare came to rule my days and render the prospect of sleep terrifying. This nightmare consisted of me walking downstairs within my kindergarten. It wasn't exactly my kindergarten, mind you: the rooms were too big and too empty, containing no desks or chairs. Faint whispers of children could be heard from the otherwise silent ducts, and the walls were crammed full of clocks whose faces bore no numbers yet ticked all the same.

In this dream I walked alone, but often turned to check if any pursuers stalked me. Without any sense of goal or destination, I found myself pushing through a heavy door and entering a yawning, concrete stairwell. A yellow janitor sign featuring the injured-looking and fractured silhouette of a man informed me: *Stairs Closed*. But it only blocked the way up.

So, placing my hand along the grimy rail, I descended. I went down and down, and at the base stood only a small, child-sized door, one that an adult would need to crouch to fit though. It was painted red. Somehow, I understood it was unlocked, and that it led to...somewhere. Somewhere horrible. I understood nothing else about it, but the door inspired within me not trepidation, nor mere nervousness, but real fear.

Did it conceal devils—or giant spiders? No, nothing so specific. Nothing that could be defined. What this door concealed was a force absent of love and light. It was a quivering, pulsating presence that suffocated my heart and polluted me with toxic, mind-altering dread. This force would never open the door. It would never pounce, nor ensnare me in its sticky tendrils. At least, not yet. All it would do is wait, and wait...as long as it would take...into my adulthood, maybe...or into my final moments, prostrate in my deathbed...for the day to come when I chose to tell the door: *I am ready for you to open.*

All the next week when I tried explaining, the adults only laughed. They patted me on the head and informed me from hideous mouths that *nightmares aren't real.* The adults were impotent to make sense of that horrific and very real sensation caused by the presence that I knew lived beyond the little red door.

That is the feeling you must cause in your enemies. You must return them to childhood and remove their sense of logic and coherence, so they once again wet the proverbial bed. You must punish them for assuming the universe organizes itself around them, or is organized at all. You must transport them to...

THE NIGHTMARE REALM

The cabinet stood on its own, opposite from Laird on the other end of the aisle. I fabricated it of the same substance as that of my erstwhile nightmare door, and it likewise appeared quite small, like an item from the world's most depressing children's playset.

The papers released from Laird's arms, legs, and mouth. This must have provided some relief to his limbs, as they'd been gripping down nearly to the point of crushing his bones. The papers still floated nearby, threateningly, but a single sheet fell to his feet as if dropped from the ceiling. This sheet contained no life as the others did. In fact, it was one of the sheets I'd filled out for him that day, and the data it requested, it said, would be located...straight ahead.

Laird trembled. The little, red filing cabinet captured his attention like a monument intruding upon our world from an alien plane of existence. He knew he needed to access it. Drawing closer, he perhaps perceived it to be not built of any familiar substance. Its structure was rigid like steel, but its surface quivered.

Quivering steel. Quivering with anticipation.

The little cabinet was hungry.

Its bottom drawer opened in greeting, friendly as a handshake. *Come forward*, it seemed to say. *Everything you seek is inside my mouth.*

Laird stepped forward as if approaching a canyon, and he gazed into the tunnel within the monstrous cabinet. It revealed no mere enclosure for hanging file folders, but an inky darkness that swallowed the dim overhead lights. Now Laird really doubted where his career had taken him, but as he turned to abscond, the same papers he'd trusted his entire life acted as a collective and formed a wall.

In a desperate move, Laird threw himself into it but failed to break through to the other side. Its rubbery, sticky surface urged him backward, toward his destiny.

Desperate for a clue, his attention became fixated on the cabinet's open maw. Wordlessly, it beckoned. As he bent closer to peer into the darkness, he found the cabinet had grown—or perhaps he'd shrunk? In either case, his sides scraped painfully along the drawer's jagged edges. First went his feet, and he received the impression that they were no longer of this world. They were in a bad place, where the rest of him would soon join. The same sensation occurred for his pelvis, his torso and arms, and his wrinkly neck. Eventually, his whole body arrived at a location where there existed nothing...nothing besides darkness and dirty fingers.

7

THE PESKY QUESTION OF THE LAW

Seminar after seminar, attendees ask the same question, and it's one that points to an enormous, collective misconception among human beings everywhere: *what is the legality of murder?*

Dear Reader, I'll give you the short answer before I give you the long. The law doesn't care if you murder people. This can be understood with three simple points:

1. **The law doesn't care if you murder people**
2. **The law doesn't care if you murder people**
3. **The law doesn't care if you murder people**

From my own veracious narrative, we've already witnessed the law's indifference to Harold smashing that pedestrian on the street. And likewise, no agent of any jurisdiction batted an eye when I electrocuted Cody. And as it would turn out, they wouldn't care about Laird, either. At least, not in any urgent way that might disrupt business.

For evidence, look no further than our current President. You'd think with all the members of our esteemed press, as well as the all-seeing eye of the public, such a high-ranking politician would face legal repercussions for terminating an oh-so precious human life. Yet it is documented Bill Clinton staged the suicide of Vince Foster, making it appear as if the hapless attorney put a handgun into his mouth and pulled the trigger. In fact, Clinton's cronies hired their own cronies to assassinate Foster and dump his body in the park, hand still gripping the gun.

And what consequences did Clinton face? Why, only to become one of the most rich, successful, and fellated men in history.

Or, take my hometown of Baltimore (I call it my hometown, though up until my recent brush with the inner-city witch, I'd only set foot within it less than a dozen times). According to reports, 325 individuals were murdered in Baltimore in 1995—a rate that had remained more or less steady for the preceding five years. Of those, the police classified only 47% of the cases as solved. And anyone who knows how statistics play out in the real world understands that figure to be exaggerated.

FUN FACT:

over 494 million firearms were sold to Americans between 1899 and 1996!

Don't get me wrong, plenty of agencies exist to pantomime caring about murder, but it is only an elaborate act of theater. For the most part, these killings don't effect or bother anybody in law, and no particularly impressive effort is invested—by the same species responsible for agriculture and the rocket ship, mind you—in halting this constant cycle of bloodshed and sorrow.

Nonetheless...

YOU MAY NEED TO TANGO WITH A COUPLE COPS FROM TIME TO TIME

I'd gone home after my makeover, exhausted from the mall walking and apparition summoning. Wednesday morning, I arrived at work in my new, all-black get up. It was quite the showstopper. The front desk girl gasped. An accountant dropped his powdered donut. Security even tried stopping me in the lobby, before they realized my identity and bowed with embarrassment.

Lance, ever the perfect secretary, clapped upon my arrival into our suite. "Love it," he gushed, rising to meet me and examining my look from all sides, dusting my shoulder here and there. "It's Dana Scully meets Morticia Adams meets...the greater Lutherville business community?"

"Thank you, my friend," I said. "What's the news?"

Much as it displeased both of us, he needed to change directions from my bold fashion. "You've been getting calls from the police department all morning," he said. "I tried ignoring them, and tried to explain you're too important to answer their boring, stupid questions—"

"Did you actually use those words with the police?"

"Yes, of course."

"Good boy."

"But they sounded real insistent. I think they're coming here to speak with you."

That's when a knock at the office door interrupted. We turned to see a substantially built woman standing just outside, in the hall. She wore tan slacks, as well as a white polo beneath a brown sports coat. A shield-shaped golden badge was attached to her belt, peeking out from behind the coat's hem.

"Good morning. How are you?" she said, by way of introduction. Her magenta lipstick contrasted with her brown skin in a way that did not quite work, and her mouth curled into an enormous smile meant to convey friendliness and authority. "Hope I'm not interrupting an important business meeting. I know you office types keep busy schedules."

"As a matter of fact, you are interrupting," Lance interjected. "We were just discussing—"

I waved him off. "It's okay, Lance. Let this one go." I gestured him back to his seat, then squinted my attention at our intruder. "You'll have to excuse my assistant," I said diplomatically. "He's just doing his job. Anyway, my name is Jenny Johnston."

Her wrist flopped as she pointed at me. "Of course I know who *you* are. You think I just walk around random office buildings, looking for people to bother? County PD's not that slow. It's me who should be doing the introduction, and my name is Darnelle Rockamore."

She walked into the room and extended her hand, taking my own in her impressive grip.

"Nice to meet you, Ms. Rockamore."

"That's Detective Rockamore, for your information." She pointed toward my office. "Why don't we take a couple minutes to discuss a matter in private?"

I huffed. "Would it be possible to get something down on the calendar, instead?"

She shook her head and gave me a dismissive finger-wiggle. "Too busy? For the police? Tell your appointment you'll be a little late. If they don't understand, well, tell 'em they can talk to me about it."

She did not intimidate me, and with less effort than a finger snap, I could have banished her to the building's rooftop. But I found myself curious as to what sort of questions she had in mind, and so assented to speak and we went inside.

I closed the door behind me and sat behind my desk. Darnelle casually poked around, observing my showcase table of crystal business awards, then glancing at the contents of my desk: my rolodex, my computer, my pen stand, and my Garfield mug full of pens (yes, I really like pens). "I hope everything is okay," I told her. "It's not every day that someone from the police office stops by unannounced."

Still standing, she gazed out the window at the ongoing traffic of York Road. "What? Oh, yeah, everything's good. I mean, your coworker died in a freak electrocution accident on Monday, which is horrific, but other than that—say, who's this?"

Interrupting herself, she grabbed a silver-framed photograph off my side dresser. It featured two girls seated on a bench eating ice cream. "Nice picture. This you and your sister?"

I crossed my arms.

"Are you the older looking one, or is that her?"

"She was the older one."

Detective Rockamore nodded. Perhaps feeling awkward, she took the opportunity to sit, and performed an exaggerated show of making herself comfortable, leaning backward almost to the point of slouching and crossing one long leg over the other like a man. I supposed she spent most of her professional time with men, as I did, and in this way felt kinship toward her.

"It's a good company you work for, Mrs. Johnston," she said. "Nobody seems too bent out of shape about the accident—or what we *assume* is an accident. Everyone

I spoke with on my way in this morning has been real accommodating."

"Of course. We want to be compliant with the law at all times. May I ask, have you spoken with many KLR employees?"

"A reasonable amount, yes. Just to gauge the temperature."

"Did any of them say anything about me?"

My question confused Rockamore, who must not have been accustomed to subjects turning the conversation toward themselves. "Would you expect them to say something about you?"

"No. Yes? I don't know. I'm just curious if they did, and if so, whether or not they liked my hair."

"Ah ha. No, none of that. Mostly, they told me they thought it all a little strange, that one of your coworkers was reported missing by his wife last night—one that you work with closely, in fact. Had you heard that he'd gone missing?"

"Wow, that's terrible. I had no idea," I feigned, giggling at the quaint wording of Laird being *missing*, when in fact he'd been banished into a wholly different and more terrible plane of existence. "Which one? Is it Vance, that old alley cat?"

She pulled a little notebook from her coat pocket. "Laird Ott, Director of Operations Management. Did you see him at all yesterday?"

"Why yes. Though it was just routine business. If he meant to skip town or call out sick, he said none of it to me."

"How would you characterize Mr. Ott?"

I rolled my eyes. "Characterize? Detective, you're assuming that the man has any character in the first place. I don't know much about him at all, except that he is obsessed with paperwork—"

Darnelle raised an eyebrow and jotted something in her notebook. I craned my neck forward to see, but she held it away from me. "Let me think," I demurred, then closed my eyes. Using my newfound omniscience, I looked over her shoulder, and saw written on the line in her blue pen: *Johnston has opinions.*

When I opened my eyes, I found her staring directly at me. "Well?" she said. "Come up with anything?"

"No, unfortunately, and I'm afraid I'm very busy. If you don't have more questions, then I'll wish you luck and respectfully ask that you take your leave."

"Sure, sure. I understand. Lots of meetings and whatnot—an important phone call, a big lunch date? But let me ask one more thing. Were you at all surprised by the death of Cody McMillain?"

"Not at all. He was a total klutz."

"Bad luck, huh? What a shame. Can strike anyone, at any time." The detective's snarky tone didn't match the words—not exactly—and she stood, then dropped her business card on my desk, tapping the number beneath her name. "If you think of anything, give my office a call, will you?"

Before exiting completely, she lingered at my door. "Oh, and speaking of terrible things, are you close to your neighbors?"

"The Kieslings? God, no."

"They've been struck with bad luck as well. Had to commit their own son to the loony bin, said he was hallucinating and hysterical."

"Detective Rockamore, am I part of some investigation? And does it include the private matters of my neighbors?"

Now it was her turn to feign. "That's preposterous. My department just keeps tabs on these sorts of things."

"Well, it's unfortunate to hear, but doesn't surprise me. They're overbearing toward the boy." As soon as the words passed my lips, I realized that the expressed knowledge indicated *some* level of closeness between my household and the Kieslings.

If Darnelle noticed this slip, she didn't let on. She instead switched gears quite drastically, "You know, my sister passed away, too. I was sixteen, she was eighteen."

"That was our ages, too," I said, becoming slightly choked up.

Rockamore returned to my side desk, taking another look at the photo. "We grew up in East Baltimore," she said. "Beautiful city, but there's parts where nobody should go. Haunted parts."

That made me flinch. In her previous two statements, she'd not only revealed something deeply personal, but uttered a cryptic comment that would have sounded like lunacy a week ago, but today made so much sense. I stammered, but she required no response. She proceeded past Lance out of the suite, and called to us both, "I'll be in touch. And stay safe out there, y'all. Who knows what kinda bad luck's just lurking around the corner."

Dear Reader, remember: before that week, I'd never really killed any coworkers, and knew not what powers the law did or did not possess over the lives of white collar laborers. The law is effective in this way, I must admit. It holds sway within the collective imaginations of homicide virgins, forcing them to question whether to indulge their deliciously violent fantasies.

Lance popped in. "Everything okay? Your new look is arresting, but I didn't think it qualified you for actual jail."

"I'm not sure, but no worries for now, Lance. Keep an

ear to the ground, will you?"

"You know I will. Can I get you a coffee?"

We shared a good at laugh at that, then I shut the door and sat in my seat. I closed the blinds and turned off all lights in the office save for my desk lamp, so that I was surrounded with darkness.

As we say in the business world, there were a lot of moving pieces, and I needed to keep close watch over everything. As far as the KLR Division Heads were concerned, there was two down, and two to go, plus that pesky consultant.

I closed my eyes and projected my vision outward.

WHAT DID THE OTHER DIVISION HEADS THINK?

While intrepid Detective Rockamore strutted the halls of KLR in search of witnesses, Phillip Platt and Hank Domino had just started a private tête è tête in Hank's office. Their strung out appearances surprised me—especially Hank's, whose hair looked barbarically unkempt. His forehead vein rippled up from between his eyes to his hairline like a rain-swollen earthworm. Guess the meditation and herbal tea hadn't kicked in yet.

"C'mon Hank, you gotta admit, it's getting real uncool around here." Not in its usual ponytail, Philip's hair was likewise disheveled, and sweat visibly soaked into his shirt beneath his armpits. "The restructure or whatever it's called is scheduled Monday. Cody's six feet under, Laird's on the lam, and Harold's practically catatonic, which wasn't even part of the master plan! Plus, now there's detectives casing the joint. *Detectives!* I mean, you don't know anything about this, right?"

Hank shook his head.

"And I sure don't, which means we're out of the loop. Man, there's a murderer loose! Oh God, and one of us will be next." Phillip reached into his coat pocket and withdrew a tiny bottle of whiskey, which he proceeded to shakily pour into his styrofoam coffee cup. He offered the dregs to Hank, who waved it away.

"No, never touch the stuff," he said, ever the puritan. Hank massaged his temples, contemplating, and after a moment his forehead vein shrunk away. He was visibly very stressed but did a better job of reigning it in around others. "Alright, alright, calm down. We can figure this out using logic."

"Logic? Man, screw that. Tell Laird about logic! He's probably tied up and ball-gagged in someone's trunk—"

Hank reached out and took Philip by the arm, guiding the cup up to his lips. Philip sipped it like a baby and let his breathing decelerate. "Logically," Hank began. "All we know is what we've been told, which is that Harold got sick, Laird went missing, and Cody had an accident."

"Accident, right. You and I both know Jenny offed him."

"We know nothing of the sort, Phil."

"Have you seen her today? She's dressed up all in black, like the goddamned grim reaper. I swear to God she's coming for one of us next."

Hank nodded. Though Philip acted unhinged, Hank must have seen some truth embedded in his paranoia. "For argument's sake, let's consider your hypothesis. Say Jenny intends on assassinating us, one by one. First of all, remember who we're talking about. This is Jenny Johnston, not Jason Vorhees, and she can wear all the black clothes and makeup she wants, as well as dye her hair and all the rest. That still doesn't change the fact that she is, on a good day, an incompetent twat."

The two men shared a laugh at that, as did I. Dear Reader, if you have never before spied on your coworker's secret meetings, I highly recommend it. Take it from someone with oodles of experience: it is so mentally and emotionally freeing when you finally have proof that when your coworkers congregate, their conversation invariably descends into foulmouthed insults toward you.

DOES IT HURT AT FIRST...

... to hear them openly gossip of how they despise you?

I must admit it stung, yes. But only that first time. Later, after I'd become more accustomed to mystical eavesdropping, hearing them became a pleasant part of my daily routine, one that reinforces the fact that other people are awful and obliterating them is justifiable and the only sane solution.

Think of your own workplace and the meetings that occur without you present. I guarantee that—probably right now—those malcontents are:

- **Forming plots to tarnish your reputation**
- **Devising schemes to offload their trivial responsibilities onto you**
- **...and sometimes even planning how they'd kill you right back!**

To that last point's end, Hank calmly stood and walked to his desk. He bent and opened its bottom drawer, and withdrew two alloy-framed, Ruger revolvers. He popped the clip of one to demonstrate to Philip that it was loaded, then flipped it so that he held it by the barrel and offered it to his colleague. "Ever fired one of these before?"

Philip grabbed the gun. "Hell yeah, but I don't usually carry heat around the office."

"You absolutely should. Especially now, as things are starting to get a little, as you say, uncool. I need you and you need me. Think carefully. If we can squeeze through this in one piece, we'll arrive on the other side of next week's merger as legacy division heads."

"With leverage for some serious salary negotiations."

"That's correct, my friend."

The two men were relative strangers and had little in common. But, as dayjobs so often force people to do, they joined in alliance against a common crisis. Hank cocked the revolver and holstered it beneath his coat. "If that black-clad bitch tries anything, don't wait."

"No way, dude. If she comes at me with a toaster, I'm pulling this bad boy straight out, then blammo. All it takes is one perfect shot."

Again, they both laughed, the talk of shooting me easing their minds. "But don't just look out for Jenny," Hank advised. "There's another member of the fairer sex who might be responsible for our current outbreak of workplace drama."

Philip's eyes glimmered. "I thought that, too. What's Eva doing up there on floor ten, anyway? There might be bigger forces at play than we realize."

"So it would seem, so it would seem." Hank patted his counterpart on the shoulder somewhat paternally, then raised a warning finger. "For the time being, I need you calm, focused, and highly alert. Remember, Philip: anything is possible."

...WHICH IS TRUER THAN MOST PEOPLE REALIZE

Before I turned sixteen, my father still spoke to me, and one of his oft-repeated tales from his own youth went like this:

"I didn't have any experience," he'd brag at the dinner table to me and Carol. "No resumé. Never really held a job with real responsibilities, either. I went to trade school but didn't have any kind of fancy degree like kids need nowadays. But I made up for it in character. Want to know what I did?"

"What, Dad?" we would respond, on cue.

And he'd continue, "I marched right into that office and shook the hand of the lady at the front desk. And I demanded—politely of course, that's important—to speak with the hiring manager. And when she told me he was in a meeting, want to know what I said?"

"What, Dad?"

"I said, 'that's fine with me.' And I took a seat in the lobby and let her know I'd be ready and waiting whenever he was. I only needed fifteen minutes of his time. That was twenty years ago. And now look at us. Huge house, two cars, and I'm sending both of you to college and taking care of your mother—all on one salary. And speaking of college, Carol, were you leaning Princeton or..."

What Dad thought he taught us was a life lesson about confidence. I suppose that's true. But underneath his unremarkable tale lay a deeper message, one whose depth revealed itself only after I became older. It is this: we shape reality with our minds.

My father knew he wanted the job at that company, and he went after it. The inclination to do so germinated internally and manifested itself as action. That is but one example, and I include it because it is self-evident and easily grasped by laypeople such as yourself, Dear Reader.

What my clients often fail to realize is that all reality can be manipulated according to our desires. After Denise infused me with the powers of the old gods, I learned that the physical world with which we interact is but a cloth, and it rests atop a plastic, malleable material—if you will—a wet, black clay of sorts, full of diamond flecks and bits of bone. Once you see it, you can play with it. Mold it. Form it into any image, of this world or another. All it takes is the ability to visualize the changes.

Dear Reader, I can hear your grumbling. *I was born with a x, y, or z disadvantage,* or *I believe nature dictates will,* or *I don't posses the power of the old gods.* If you have learned one thing from my book so far, I hope it is to quit making excuses. Everything that exists in your life orig-inates from within your mind: your surroundings, your friends, your sense of fulfillment. All of it. Look anywhere else to change your circumstances and you will only waste your time and sigh.

But What of the Consultant?

I'd rejoin with Hank and Philip soon, but their mention of Eva returned that consultant to my mind, and I scanned the building to find her.

As Philip raced back to the IT department, Eva was just entering the building's lobby. As I've stated, she was quite the sight to behold, and though not much intimidates me, I found her unique beauty genuinely off-putting. Why men of our era continually lust after such skinny figures, I'll never understand. What do you even hold onto? And if they turn sideways, what do you even see?

In any case, the males occupying the lobby either bowed to her or obnoxiously whistled as Eva's clicking heels carried her past them and toward the elevators.

Just then, Darnelle Rockamore turned the corner and practically bumped straight into Eva, who tried maneuvering around the detective to no avail. "Ah, Ms. LeFey—love the name—I need a minute of your time."

Their bodies shifted back and forth like dueling WNBA players, then Eva finally managed to jump around Darnelle and stab the elevator button with her manicured finger. "I don't have a minute, Miss..."

"It's Detective Rockamore, and no worries, I'll follow you."

They entered the elevator.

"As you're aware, there's been an unusual uptick in odd occurrences in KLR, which for sake of time I won't recount. But I assume that you can tell me, Eva, what is the nature of The Nameless Corporation's consultancy? Because nobody else can."

I tried to gauge Eva's facial expression, but found it oddly blurry, as if obscured behind smoky glass. But everything else within that elevator appeared clear as Crystal Pepsi, including the detective herself, who stared inquisitively at her subject.

"My superior has issued specific guidelines about dealing with the law, and I'm not required to answer," Eva replied. "If your rinky-dink police department wishes to pry into our restructuring, I suggest contacting Internal Affairs."

"*Rinky dink?* Now hold on, Ms. LeFey. You don't have to respect my agency, but you do need to respect the law, and I will not be talked down to, especially when I'm being so polite and personable. Let me ask you again: what is the nature of your business? And while we're at it, tell me who contracted you to consult with KLR...this superior you speak of."

But she received no reply, which surprised me not at all. The doors opened to the tenth floor. She followed Eva into the spartan lobby of the consultant's operations—the area preceding the restricted zone—where my own explorations always cut short. Eva strolled past her gruff security guards without another word and disappeared behind a massive door. Rockamore chatted up the stoic guards, but they insisted they'd need to see a warrant.

I tried peering into the heart of the tenth floor to observe Eva but found it impossible. When I cast my vision forward through that door, it became stuck. I saw no farther than anyone else. I searched around the walls for a weak spot to penetrate, but Eva's operations remained hidden behind some spectral cloak. This confused me, as I could see everywhere else that I wished.

But for the time being, my schedule was too jam-packed for such diversions. I saved Eva for last and prepared for Thursday's critical agenda item.

8

ACCRUE ENDLESS DEBT

Oh, what a wonderful pastime, sitting around and thinking of ways to torture your coworkers. That's what I did in my office all the next morning. My visions were so real, part of me questioned if I'd actualized them by mistake. One challenge high level dark magic users face is discerning the subtle line between fantasy and reality.

But then a sound interrupted me, and I woke from my vivid trance. What I'd heard came from the direction of my closet. Then it happened a second time: *rustling*.

No sound at all usually comes from my closet, let alone one signaling a living thing. Had KLR slipped so downhill as to attract rats or raccoons? No matter how many destructive acts I oversee, little furry critters always give me the heebie-jeebies.

Again, more insistently, came the uninvited sound. I stood but hesitated, stalled by indecision, and shuddered at the thought of a rodent's gummy feet scuttling across the new, black open-toed shoes I'd selected that morning.

But...what if something worse lay concealed behind the door? What if I'd accidentally summoned something bad during my reverie? Something not easily controlled. As Hank stated and my experience proved, *anything*, truly, is possible. The nightmare-being of my childhood might have finally arrived from beyond the veil of sanity. Nonetheless, a force compelled me to approach the door.

I gripped the knob and turned.

Beyond lay nothing: no umbrellas, no shoes, no curated arrangement of coats for every occasion. No rodents. All of my usual belongings were replaced, instead, by a black, fathomless void.

If the closet retained any of its interior dimensions, I no longer discerned them. If I stepped forward, I might step off a precipice and float away. From out of this darkness, a frosty breeze greeted me, brushing a stray lock across my forehead and creeping up my pants and shirtsleeves.

Then, at a distance difficult to determine, what I took to be two gleaming eyes opened, and I gripped the closet door to keep from buckling forward. They were radioactive green, luminous as neon. Beholding them, I knew myself to be visited by an infernal entity.

"Jenny Johnston," spoke its voice—deep, weary, made of the frosty breeze. Saying my name, the syllables trailed off and echoed. Whether male or female was irrelevant, for it could not be human. "I am known by those of your plane as N'thydolarp. Through the ritual, I have been summoned, and you must prepare me a sacrifice. The powers flowing through you come at a price, and when we next meet, I shall make my demand."

I nodded. "It's nice to meet you, N'thydolarp. May I ask a follow-up question?"

It took a few seconds to answer. "Ask."

"When would be the latest date you'd want this sacrifice?"

"End of week."

"Great, I'll be sure to make a note of that. And real quick, what kind of sac—"

But its two glowing eyes dissolved into nothingness. The dark repopulated with physical objects: the walls, the hangers, my various fashionable belongings. Yet the return of the canny couldn't erase the demon's presence, nor its penetrating stare. I thought back to the hair-raising sensation of being watched I'd felt on Denise's block the night Harold and I hit the man, and I wondered if this entity had been spying on us then. Perhaps it always did, all the time, just as a supervisor spies every action of their charges.

And Denise had alluded to a sacrifice, come to think of it, one for her "old gods." But in my hastiness, I'd neglected to ask for elaboration. Did it matter? Probably.

A shadow of doubt spread across my mind like the Gulf War oil spill. I suddenly felt very unmoored and uncertain in my actions and decisions. N'thydolarp's arrival marked a new urgency, so I hastened along with my business plan for...

UNSHAKEABLE, UNBREAKABLE HANK

Hank the zen-master. Hank, calm as a clam. When I next checked in, his eyes peeked from above the rim of a mug of herbal tea as he walked at a moderate rate on his office treadmill. He pulled a mini tape recorder from his pocket and spoke aloud, "Look into lunch with Jenny Johnston tomorrow. It's impossible that she's responsible for Laird's disappearance, but she may yet know more about it. Desperate as she is for friendship, she'll spill the beans. And if not, well...I can be very persuasive."

Having settled upon his plan, he grabbed a workout bag that he'd brought with him that morning, and made sure to pack his revolver in its side pocket (which is what he referred to when reminding himself of his persuasiveness). Then he exited, telling his assistant he was heading to the gym to—ugh—*blow off some steam.*

He claimed he'd be back in the afternoon.

In his sky-blue BMW sedan, Hank cruised down York Road, passing car washes and gas stations and chain restaurants and local restaurants with their marquee signs advertising happy hours and steak nights. He passed strip mall after strip mall of liquor stores and electronics outlets and interior design stores, as well as big box stores and grocery stores. He passed doctor's offices and a couple schools and many random buildings full of office space for companies of which no one has ever heard.

For the first couple minutes, his thoughts consumed him, but while stopped at a light, he hit play on the BMW's tape deck. The song filtering through in surround sound featured an effeminate male singer mewling after some object of affection, and the lyrics resonated with Hank, by the looks of how he soulfully warbled along. When the chorus came, both he and the singer simultaneously intoned: *"You come crash, into me."*

He pulled into the parking lot, snatched his bag from the backseat, and proceeded into the sprawling single story gym. Hank greeted the front desk staff the same way he would any stranger: no eye contact and an offhand wave. Once dressed in his short shorts, sneakers, and brightly colored headband, he stalked out to the floor to pump iron and get sweaty.

Hank's whole image was one of cool, calm control.

This meant underneath his public persona lay a vast ocean of stress that could only be resolved through self-inflicted physical punishment. As far as I know, the stress didn't come from any real place. For example, he lacked for no material comfort and the responsibilities of his job—like all jobs—were negligible. Perhaps childhood trauma from a demanding father vexed his psychology. I'll never know because I never got the chance to sit down with him and ask.

His exercise routine fascinated me. To work up a sweat, he climbed onto a Stairmaster, which to my eyes resembled a Medieval torture device. He then thrust himself onto a stationary bicycle and blasted away, turning up the volume of his Walkman and listening to a brassier, obnoxious tune from the same tape. The cardio work represented a mere prelude for the weight room, where the beast became truly unleashed. Hank grunted and screamed his way beneath the barbells, garnering concerned glances from other nearby men.

Letting him live might have been crueler than killing him.

But this wasn't about him. It was about mc.

Hank hopped off the sweaty black cushion of the lifting seat, then went to grab a cone of water. The cooler glugged as he lifted the spigot's handle, and his reflection in one of the giant mirrors captured his attention. Admiring his own physique distracted him from the appearance and temperature of his water until he sipped and spit it out, disgusted. It wasn't water at all, but hot black coffee.

This phenomenon would perplex anyone else, as the cooler appeared to contain only water. But so preoccupied was Hank's mind that he didn't give a second thought to whether this event came to life through supernatural interference. Instead, he moved in the direction of what would calm him: a staff member to berate.

CHANCE ENCOUNTERS

Meanwhile, Detective Rockamore waited for a hot dog at the Towson Town Mall food court. Her investigation intrigued me, and since I assumed she believed me a top suspect, I kept an eye on her.

She happened to spot Lance walking past, his arms full of bags from Tommy Hilfiger and Guess. She waved him over and he approached cautiously. "Aren't you on the clock young man?"

"Jenny doesn't care how long a lunch I take."

"In that case, let me buy you lunch."

Lance wouldn't want to spend any time with a detective, but since he remained (at that point) oblivious to my involvement in the strange events around the office, the siren call of a free hot dog ensnared him. Plus, all that shopping must have made him tired, and he'd appreciate a chance to sit. Once his order came up, the unlikely duo slid into the booth with the least amount of dried soda covering its plastic seats.

"Your boss is quite the woman," Rockamore said between chews. "But her coming to work dressed in black is a new development, right?"

"Do you always talk with your mouth full?"

That stunned Rockamore. She shut her mouth and made an exaggerated show of finishing her bite, while Lance giggled. "I'm only kidding," he said, and my heart swelled a bit seeing him deflect the detective's probing.

Their chitchat meandered, covering Rockamore's general experience; she spent fifteen years as a patrolman in

East Baltimore, around where she grew up, then transferred to County PD. "I don't know which I like better," she said. "But while it's no walk in the park, the county life is much, much easier. I deal with people like the employees at KLR. People who've never really experienced hardship, like your boss."

Lance squeezed a dribble of ketchup from one of a handful of packets, and shrugged. "Oh, Jenny's experienced plenty of hardship. More than most, for sure."

"Oh?" Something about Lance's comment amused her very slightly. "How so?"

"Well for starters, she had a bad childhood. Her sister passed away early in an accident."

"Right. I gathered that," said Rockamore. The two continued eating in silence, and I forgave Lance for this lapse in discretion. All of the sugar, oil, and sodium flowing through his system must have made him a little loopy. "Do we know how?"

Lance shook his head. "Some kind of accident, but she never talks about it."

After eating, Lance thanked Rockamore for the lunch and she said *anytime* in a way that communicated *never again*. As he gathered his oversized bags and started to walk away, she called after him, "Young man. Be safe out there."

"Don't worry about me," he said. "Us county folk are tougher than you think."

And again, something about his comment made her smile. "Sure. But you have my number. Call me if anyone from KLR is in danger, will you?"

Rockamore glanced at her pager as it went off but didn't head toward the payphones. She headed instead toward Sally's Stylez.

And Back at The Gym

...Hank was still thirsty.

"I'm sorry," said the polo-shirted clerk behind the counter. "I don't know what happened. It gives water to everyone else."

"Listen," said Hank. He leaned forward and kept his voice low and threatening. Perhaps he thought fondly of his gun as his face settled into the cold, grim, expression of a serial killer recounting his worst childhood memories. "My body is a perfectly balanced machine. It is a Swiss watch. It is the Saturn Moon Rocket. And even a tiny sip of caffeine can throw off its internal calibration. My annual check-up is next week, and you better believe that if my doctor finds any irregularity to my heartbeat, I'm suing this gym into oblivion. That's within my right, know that? And what is your name, young man?"

After the boy told him, he gave Hank a few quarters, so he'd go away. Hank took them across the gym lobby to the soda machine. He plugged them into the coin slot, punched in the code, then grabbed a bottle of Aquafina. He immediately opened it and took a sip but winced at its odd taste. Bottled water always has a plasticky aftertaste, but he must have noticed an unusual minerality in this instance, as if spiked with rock salt. Undeterred, he stalked toward the showers to rinse and prepare for what he believed would be a busy afternoon of meetings back at KLR.

When Hank emerged from the steamy shower, he found himself alone. No workers emptied the trash cans, no fellow gym-goers quipped or bragged about their exploits. He didn't even hear the telltale sound of rubber soles squeaking over the floor.

Convinced of the locker room's emptiness, he took the opportunity to remove his towel, and beheld himself in the bathroom mirror. Such grandeur. What woman could resist? He wasn't in particularly great shape if you ask me, but that's not how he perceived the man in the reflection.

Water bottle still in hand, he went into the locker area but had trouble locating his own. He looked around as if he'd lost track of his BMW in an expansive parking lot. Confused, Hank searched for another minute among the endless rows. He must have decided to ask for help at the front desk, but...odd. Not only could he not find his belongings, but he'd lost track of the exit to this sprawling locker room.

Hank took a seat and unscrewed the top to his bottle, and he took another big mouthful. Liquid didn't spill into his mouth, but some fine powder. He hacked and wretched, spitting out gobs of it and his saliva, but try as he may, he'd still ingested a large quantity of the mysterious substance.

It couldn't be salt or sugar. Baking soda, perhaps, though this had a bitter and unpleasant flavor that numbed his mouth. He rushed to the sinks to wash out the horrible taste, but he'd lost track of their location, too.

You'd think among all this discombobulation and oral assault, he would be at wits' end and screaming for help. Believe it or not, by the looks of him, Hank started to feel good—no, great. Perhaps better than he'd ever felt in his entire life. For what he'd just ingested was fifteen hits worth of pure, unadulterated cocaine.

An exaggerated grin stretched his cheeks in opposite directions, and to take in more of the fluorescent light, his eyes widened into two red, veiny globes.

•

The blonde stylist's eyes, meanwhile, squinted at the picture thrust in her face. "Sure, she comes in all the time," she said, chomping away at an obscene quantity of gum. "Was here yesterday, in fact. Why—she go mental or something?"

Darnelle wasn't there to answer questions though. "Is a full black dye job a normal request at your establishment?"

The stylist thought as she applied the heated straightener to a client's wavy locks. "No, but I got no problem doing it. Kinda fun, actually. But since you're here, I should tell you she acted a little weird. Weird for her. Normally she comes in and just blabs, blabs, blabs her mouth off about her job. You would not believe how much that lady hates the coworkers wherever she works."

"That true?"

"Oh, big time. But yesterday, she was completely out of it."

"How so?"

"Just sat and stared off into space. Body was here, but mind somewhere else. It was like giving a perm to one of the Gap mannequins."

Rockamore's pager buzzed again. She thanked the stylist and exited the salon, finding a nearby row of payphones and dialing up her caller, who was apparently doing some research. She listened for a minute, nodding, and eventually the caller started to relay information about Harold. "Got it," Rockamore said. "And his car?"

"Never left his residence," spoke the tinny voice on the other end. "I did find something, though. Kind of a long shot, but a car matching his description was reported in a hit and run downtown last week."

"Where downtown?"

"East side, Ensor street—"

Rockamore cut off her assistant. "Near the cemetery?"

"Y-yes. Wait, that's your old beat, right?"

"Uh huh. Listen, pull the numbers for Hank Domino and Philip Platt, and tell them both to rush home. *Immediately.*"

•

Hank frequently called the gym his second home, so technically speaking, he was already there. Granted, under my current manipulations, the gym barely resembled itself. But Hank looked carefree, as he couldn't stop laughing and even started doing a little dance.

But he lacked music. To assist, my avatar materialized at the far end of a row of the blue lockers, outfitted in deepest black.

"Jenny! It's crazy to see you here!" Hank practically raved, licking his lips and rolling his tongue up and down in his mouth. At the very least, he still had the good sense to hold up the towel tied around his waist.

"Great seeing you too, Hank."

"I can't find the way out of this locker room," he said, exuberant tone not matching his circumstance. "Does that seem strange? By the way, this is the men's changing room. You might be lost!"

I nodded throughout these staccato observations. "Hank, you're a little edgy."

"Am I? I swallowed some powder that made me feel this way. Maybe it was heroin, or special K?" So far, the unnatural amount of dopamine flooding his system hindered his ability to think, but speaking these words aloud, their meaning impressed upon him for the first time.

"Jenny? Wait..."

My avatar extended an open palm, and a yellow Walkman with a set of black headphones appeared on it.

"Maybe listening to music might help ease your mind?" I said, offering it.

Sweat ran in rivulets down his forehead, his face reddened, and his hand moved with an insect's jitteriness as he grabbed the Walkman. "Music, yes—yes! Something to listen to would be good, something mellow and soothing. Is it Dave Matthews, or Hootie?"

"Oh, it's better," I replied. "Much better."

He slipped on the headphones and depressed the play button, wide-pupil eyes darting. What he heard did not consist of a friendly fiddle or the strum of an acoustic guitar, but a single, incredibly loud thump of a bass drum: *boom*. Then silence. Then again, *boom*. Then a voice.

His own.

She can put on all the black clothes and makeup she wants, he heard himself say. *That still doesn't change the fact that she is, on a good day, an incompetent twat.*

The music kicked in as the snippet played on repeat, an ominous dirge of noisy bass and reverb-drenched electric guitar. Hank clawed at the headphones to remove them, but found they'd painfully fused themselves into each side of his head, clamping down like oversized ticks. If he really wanted to take them off, he'd need to rip off his face.

At a certain point the song broke into a chorus of sorts, which featured another of Hank's recent quotes from his meet-up with Philip: *If that black-clad bitch tries anything, don't wait.*

Don't wait. Don't wait.

What terror feels like under the influence of so much blow, most folks can't even imagine. It certainly didn't look fun. Hank's mental and physical capabilities buckled when confronted with this fundamental rift in reality. I experienced a rush myself, watching him turn and smack straight into a wall. He reminded me of a mouse, an analogy that holds up both ways, as I had evolved into a figure as terrifying as any mouse perceives a human. Though struggling to untwist his legs, he managed to steady, then ran faster than he'd ever run before (a distinction soon to be superseded).

He rounded the corner of another row of lockers to find me standing before him yet again. I asked, with my voice pumping full volume through the headphones, "What's the big rush?"

Desperate for oxygen, his body caused him to take huge, gasping breaths. Unfortunately for him (and fortunately for me), this meant even more of the drug burrowed into the porous tissue of his throat and sinuses. Anyone who has experienced uppers will understand the famous *up* feeling comes with an expiration date, followed by a steep crash. This phenomenon befell Hank, and his face darkened into a strangulated purple. "Help me!" he pleaded—not to me, but to a God who does not exist. "Where's my gun? Where's my gun?"

Or something like that. Discerning his exact words became difficult the more he slobbered and choked.

"You want to leave, Hank?"

I gestured down the aisle.

"Well, the exit's right there."

True to my word, the door leading back to the real world shimmered into existence on the far wall. More unintelligible syllables escaped Hank's mouth as he hastened that direction.

But each step carried him no closer. To verify his position remained unchanged, he looked to me, still calmly standing by his side no matter how quickly he paced. It wasn't that I floated alongside; the floor rolled the opposite direction under his feet, like a conveyor belt.

I decided to make myself unseen. Everything else became unseen too, besides:

1. **The treadmill-acting floor...**
2. **...with a wall on either side...**
3. **...and the exit not ten feet ahead...**

...and one other thing, or many things, that Hank would soon perceive. When he realized he moved backward when not walking, he also realized that the moving floor disappeared not far behind him, trailing off into...what? As my doomy heavy metal assaulted his ears, he cast his gaze backward and saw only darkness. Within that darkness, something moved. A lot of something moved. And that is when Hank really started to run.

THE IMPORTANCE OF HUMOR IN WORKPLACE EXTERMINATIONS

So many times in life, we hold back from saying what we want or need to express to others. We fear if we reveal ourselves, people will laugh at us or think us weak. That is of course true. People do that, so it makes sense we (and by *we*, I mean *you*) bottle up our emotions and store them away in a dark cellar of the soul. When these instances occur, I suggest you turn to humor.

Is there any tense situation that a joke cannot help? One time, a previous division head made my job harder by insisting I had no authority to offer reduced prices for special clients. I met with him to detail how he was wrong, and provided concrete examples of how he would need to modify his behavior so as to get out of my way. He nodded throughout our talk, yet when next week rolled around, he continued blocking my inside deals. Clearly, I was not breaking through. So one day, I took him to lunch. He excused himself to use the restaurant's bathroom, and I flagged the waiter to order a steak for myself, and a garden salad for him. The lunches arrived soon after, and my coworker yelled, "Why did you order for me?" I reminded him of the challenges when others interfere in our business, then held up my serrated steak knife. I asked my coworker if he thought it could slice through an ear, and he said, *probably*. Then I questioned if he'd ever thought what life would be like, missing an ear.

In that instance, my joke diffused the tension while expressing my seriousness about the matter. The result? He never meddled again. In fact, he never even spoke to me again.

Another time, when my husband John still spent time at home, I asked him to remove all the old clothing he no longer wore from our closet. I explained that I needed the space, and when he suggested I use one of the other several closets throughout the house, I knew I'd need to get creative in order to get my point across. I went to his bureau (not the closet in question) and removed many of his favorite pieces. I arranged them on the lawn while he was at the local office, and covered them with gasoline. When his Lexus pulled up the driveway, I threw a match on them and watched as the golden flames danced across the grass of our front yard.

Did the HOA write us a citation about that one? Of course. And did John respect me more, after my demonstration? I'd say yes. He respected me more because he feared me more. My humor is, above all, a weapon.

Plus, there's icing on the cake. Properly employed humor not only devastates the person you prank but amuses you and enlivens your spirit. That's why I devised the trap I did for Hank. Seeing him running on that treadmill for all his life, a force bubbled deep inside me. It rumbled my guts and rattled my bones, and came out sounding like...

HA! HA! HA! HA!

A heart attack would have been a blessing for Hank, but I kept it at bay. All the pores of his body leaked sweat, rendering the floor quite slick. He gave it his all, compelled by some deeply human instinct not only to survive, but to escape the inevitable darkness.

Go on, Hank! I jeered from the sideline in between my uproarious cackling. *This is it, your time to shine! Keep rushing, champ! Keep on trying! Put in the effort and you'll make it to the door!*

And make it to the door he did. The man's physical shape paid off, and though his legs pumped like a firing piston, and he needed to reach out his hand, his fingers managed to clasp around that cool, brass doorknob before it became dislodged.

Hank's feet flew behind him. He bellyflopped to the floor and the momentum cast him backwards, hurtling into the unknown. *Does this look like the work of an incompetent twat?* I cackled. *Are you not impressed by my organizational skills?* My echoing laughter might have filled the entire universe.

The void into which Hank fell was difficult to define, and language fails to describe exactly what became of him within it. But in short, he melted into a kind of sentient goo, one capable only of consciousness and suffering. And he became stretched out in all directions, mercilessly, by the faceless denizens of that far-away dimension.

9

Feeling Good is What's Right

Sometimes you turn on the news, or engage in chitchat with some uptight know-it-all, and these outside forces would have you believe the world is burning down. They will try to tell you that the environment is eroding, that unjust wars rage across the world, and that the American population gets dumber by the minute, their minds ravaged by the instant gratification of television, film and the realistic graphics of video games.

Reader, I am here to tell you that I've been on this earth for nearly fifty years, and none of that matters one bit!

1. **Your progress is justifiable**
2. **Your opinions and behaviors are justifiable**
3. **The suffering of others does not affect you**

Yet after eviscerating Hank's soul, I caught a whiff of the 'ol Emptiness once more. I decided to drive back to Denise's hovel on the abandoned street to set some matters straight.

At a particularly long red light downtown, I saw

a beggar. It was a young white woman with dirty blonde hair (and I mean dirty in the literal sense). She looked quite skinny and frail, and her eyes contained the gloom of the undead. On the bright side, she at least had a dog, which was likewise skin and bones, but at least could not comprehend its misfortune.

I pulled over to the opposite side and observed this woman from afar. She walked up and down the street, displaying a ripped out underside of a cardboard box, upon which she'd scrawled some message about being poor, without shelter, etc. Such individuals provoke a natural disdain. Where were her parents? And who allowed her to neglect her studies?

Yet I challenged myself to feel compassion. In an alternate reality, this fate might befall my own daughter. Or even me (joking). Considering my vastly different circumstance, could I be of some assistance?

My initial instinct was to exit my car, then engage her in conversation. I'd remind her that even if she'd dropped out of high school, a GED program still remained as an option. I could tell her that gaining an economic foothold in this country is rather simple if you ask your parents or are willing to at least show up for a job.

But what if material assistance might be even more helpful than my wisdom? I decided to engage in an experiment and summoned my powers to assist the young woman. I'd materialize for her a birthday cake, a diploma, a little orange pill bottle of Prozac. I tried to provide a new pair of pants without holes in the knees. Yet nothing of the sort emerged. I closed my eyes to concentrate and pushed myself—harder and harder—yet when I opened my eyes, the world remained unchanged.

Funny, how easy it had been to inflict torment upon my

work colleagues. Doing so had been almost effortless. Yet here I tried to assist this poor wretch with nothing so grand as the fates of Laird and Hank, yet my powers proved useless. To further the experiment, I set a lower bar. Could I produce for her a single red rose, so that it might sunny up her gloomy disposition? I tried, but it failed to appear.

Some matters can't be resolved with the dark arts, I told myself. Sighing, I pulled out my purse, full of credit cards and bills. I looked first at a $20. Nice chunk of change, but too generous, to the point of being creepy. Then I considered donating $5, but she'd just blunder off and spend it on drugs, surely. In that case, how about one of my many $1 bills? I'd literally never notice the loss, and it would serve as a gesture of solidarity with the waif.

The woman spotted me from across the street and ambled my direction, sniffing a possible handout. We shared the briefest of glances before I put my purse back in my pocketbook, then hit the gas and sped through the red light.

Money doesn't help the poor. We already know this. But the sight of that beggar helped me in that it reinforced a critical truth, which is:

TRYING TO DO GOOD IS POINTLESS

Now, now. I can see you raising your hands in protest. What about the time I stood around and shouted at that protest in my 20s? What about that time I gave a saucer of milk to a stray kitten? What about this, that and the other?

Keep it to yourself, Dear Reader, because it changed nothing. Feel free to put down my book, or throw it across the room if it enhances your sense of agency, but you'll be picking it up again shortly, knowing what I say to be true.

Problems are part of life. It is not the job of the

powerful to try and stop them, or to get caught up in the drama and concerns of helpless strangers. You are not responsible for the personal shortcomings of others, or to work harder because someone else decided they didn't like to work. What *is* our job is ensuring the world's problems do not touch us, and distancing ourselves as far as possible from them. This entails blinding yourself to the suffering of the weak, while adhering to the dogmas of the cruelest available hierarchies.

With that in mind, I pulled up to Denise's house ready for answers. I parked and walked up the wobbly stoop toward her front door, knocked a few times, then tried the doorknob. It surprised me to find it unlocked and surprised me further to find the inside empty, a shattered interior made more desolate by the absence of Denise's decorations. When I shouted her name, only the scurrying of unseen critters responded.

I looked again at the house, then the entire street. Save but a few, all the houses were in a state of disrepair and fairly identical. Had I arrived at the right place? As I walked up the block, Denise peeked my way, out from a different doorway than the last time I'd visited. She gestured and headed back into the house without waiting. Had I been mistaken—or had she moved her entire operation?

The windows were boarded up with haphazard wooden planks, and the sunlight through their cracks and holes provided just enough illumination. It was quite humid, but the dust motes floating in that sun looked like snow. Using a tissue from my pocketbook, I wiped the seat Denise offered before sitting. She'd been about to enjoy some tea and offered me a cup from a stained pot. Its unpleasant, savory smell—like beef stew gone bad—hit my nose instantly, and I began to decline before pushing myself to accept. After all, this was my mentor.

"Not bad," I said, after a first sip. A little saltier and less floral than usual tea, but I could adapt. "What's the flavor?"

"You've driven all the way from the county to visit me, Jenny. What are you here to discuss?"

I set the mug down on the underside of an overturned crate. "The other day I received a visitor...from another plane of existence."

She squinted, amused. "Of course you did. After the ritual, you became his acolyte. You exist exclusively as his vessel, forevermore."

"Uh huh. Sure. But I would have appreciated these terms in more explicit detail, before going through the ritual here."

"Who do you think I am, a lawyer?"

"Point taken. But I don't really understand what it means that I am his vessel."

"I asked you if you were certain you wanted to go through with the transformation, Jenny. You told me you were."

I felt a migraine coming, accompanied by the recent memory of the young beggar at the corner. "Yes, I was certain. And I've been having the time of my life. But...they aren't limitless powers, are they? I can't really do *anything* I want. Only certain things. Denise, can you help clarify all this N'thydolarp business?"

COMPREHENDING COSMIC ENTITIES

Denise rose and led me, yet again, into a back yard. Even though we'd been in a different house, and even with my blurry memory of the blood ritual, I could have sworn that this was somehow the same back yard. The fence looked the same shade of weathered gray, and it was missing the same slat in the same place. Another crucial similarity was the presence of a beekeeping operation.

As it turned out, Denise wanted to show me her bees. This relieved me, as the last thing I needed was a second ritual. Being tethered to a single cosmic entity was quite enough, thank you.

Her bees lived and worked out of four crate-like structures that contained boxes and frames. "I am a powerful sorceress," Denise said, indicating them. "So why do you think I tend bees?"

A riddle. To help along my thinking, I stooped at a safe distance and observed the small yet impressive colony. How their flaky, gossamer wings carried their fat bodies, I'll never understand. All of them carried out their labor without question, and I observed no conflict among their ranks as they crawled in and out of the openings of their wooden empire. "Well, they're fun to look at," I ventured. "And they provide honey—which, by the way, your tea could use."

"Yes, they provide honey. But more importantly, bees remind me of my place. If a bee dies, will you lose sleep over it?"

"Naturally not."

"No. But you would enjoy the fruits of its labor, as you have mentioned. It brings sweetness to your life. The bee, however, is unaware of this. It has its own motivations, and we delude ourselves if we pretend to know them. Likewise, N'thydolarp needs honey from us. And our world, to it, is merely, no... even less than..." Vaguely, Denise gestured toward the apiary.

One of the bees bounced against my head, and its miniscule buzz zippered in my ear. I flinched and thought of slapping it, but held back my hand to avoid a sting. This added an unintended tone of annoyance to my voice. "Bees can't make choices."

"They can't?"

I watched as it traced pointless parabolas in the air. "No. Only humans can."

"How do you know that, Jenny? Have you ever asked them?"

Before I could answer, a spinning veil composed of the insects encircled me. They did this as if bidden by Denise's question. While one or two occasionally strayed from the ring, they did not fly into my face or threaten to attack. Denise spoke from the other side of the droning screen, but I heard her clearly, as if she whispered directly beside me:

"*N'thydolarp disagrees.*"

The bees dissipated in a zig-zagging explosion. After they'd parted, I found myself no longer behind the house, but in front of it, its entryway boarded over with plywood. Denise had disappeared, but several of the insects lingered like stray memories from a dream. They buzzed in the air before disappearing into the urban wasteland, guided by purposes hidden within their tiny hearts.

It was Thursday, and whatever fate awaited might break my spirit. I could waste no more time, so switched my attention to KLR's chief of wares both soft and hard.

THERE ARE LIMITS TO TECHNOLOGY

Philip took a sick day, no doubt advised by the police to lay low. When I located him, he sat at his computer in the bedroom of his split-level ranch home. Computer all day at home, computer all day at work, eh Philip? Did you ever consider all this binary code stunted the creative energy you enjoyed with your band in the past?

His house lacked decoration, and was closer to the road than I'd like, but still impressively large. He sat in an uncomfortable-looking wood chair, in boxers with legs spread and wearing an R.E.M. t-shirt. He read messages on the backend of our newfangled email system, but as my invisible avatar peered over his shoulder, I saw they didn't belong to him. A-ha, I'd caught the peeping tom! He'd installed a hidden program on my computer. My opinion of him as a loathsome troll only deepened, realizing he not only did it for the job, but as a pastime.

Dear Reader: trust me, I've murdered a lot of IT Directors, and every last one is attracted to the field to satisfy their perversity. They are all men, and all shifty voyeurs: men who wanted to spy through the windows at their neighbors undressing but lacked the balls to try; men who wanted to dig like raccoons through strangers' dirty garbage but had too much propriety to do so. Knowing this, I set a trap for Philip's exclusive reading pleasure and dropped a message into the queue. He double-clicked it open in an instant.

> *From: jjohnston@KLR.com*
> *To: lbroden@KLR.com*
> *Subject: Tell No One*
>
> *Dear Lance, the recent disappearances worry me—will HE be next to take leave of our company? A day without seeing his long, unkempt locks would cripple me (emotionally).*
>
> *Yours in Confidence,*
>
> *-jj*

Philip's office chair squeaked as he sat back, and he looked quite pleased. Now that—*that*—had been a bonafide doozy, a golden ticket, a holy grail of snooping. His churning thoughts caused his fingers to twitch, and he paced the bedroom, muttering, before heading downstairs and grab a bag of pretzels.

Snacks obtained, he returned to his computer to discover yet another message that had thus far eluded his vigilant eyes:

> *From: jjohnston@KLR.com*
> *To: lbroden@KLR.com*
> *Subject: I Want Him Bad!*
>
> *Lance,*
> *I get so moist between my legs when he tries to explain what a network is to me (if only I was smart enough to understand). If he ever asked it of me, I'd submit to his whims completely.*
> *-jj*

Philip chuckled and clapped at that. "Get in line, lady," he said to the empty room. "Take a ticket and get in line."

His phone rang, startling him. I guess it didn't happen much. Imagination no doubt bubbling with adolescent imagery of the carnal variety, he grabbed it. "Platt here."

"Hey-y-y, Mr. Platt. Good to hear your voice," said Rockamore.

"You mean good to hear I'm alive. Any news?"

"Was gonna ask you the same. No word from Mr. Ott or Mr. Domino?"

"Not yet. But on my end, let's just say I've stumbled upon a juicy little tidbit you'll have to see to believe. Listen, Detective—about what we talked about earlier—I don't think it's her anymore. It's the other one."

"Yeah? Sounds like something put you in a good mood."

"Sure did. Can you come to my place?"

"Over on Seminary? Yeah, but I'm heading downtown first to check in on an old friend. Just so you know, I've got my own hunch about the perpetrator. I'll explain later, but this reminds me of a couple of the cases I used to work back in the day."

"Okay. Talk later," said Philip, not asking for clarification, though Rockamore's hunch certainly intrigued me.

After they hung up, something remarkable occurred. I wish I could take credit for it, but, Dear Reader, even I lack the deviousness to program what happened next. Of his own accord, Philip plopped back into his seat and pulled up Microsoft Office '97. I watched with fascination as he started typing, and as the words populated the white space on his monitor, I wished for a bucket of hot buttered popcorn. He wrote:

> *Dear Jenny,*
>
> *Seeing you in your new goth outfit only confirmed my feelings. As you have no doubt observed, I am a man that speaks my mind. When I want something, I go after it, and I want you. Take my hand, my nocturnal queen. Let us stir up the passions of—*

Philip was interrupted. Suddenly, there appeared in the bottom right of his screen an animated figure of a paperclip with two bulbous eyes. Though it wiggled and gyrated its lithe body, Philip had to admit it was a particularly unsexy little fella. He dismissed it with a click, then returned to his letter:

> *—let us stir up the passions of the stars, and listen while laying in grass of the graveyard for the vibrations of Saturn's r—*

Again, rather insistently, the paperclip blinked into existence, interrupting his florid outburst. Above it opened a text box which filled with the following. *It looks like you're writing a letter. Would you like some help?*

10

THE OTHER OLD GODS

While Philip dealt with the paperclip, Detective Rockamore walked through the large front door of a downtown church. Many of Baltimore's churches were huge, visually striking structures, featuring tall bell towers and spires, fashioned of impressive stone. On the other hand, I've seen others built into garages, with fold-out chairs for pews.

This particular church split the difference, being medium-sized and needing a new paint job. From the outside it didn't look particularly gothic or impressive, but its inside was full of light. Its windows weren't stained glass, but were large and open, letting in a little of the much-needed breeze. An old man seated at the front played an organ, and was the wide open space's sole resident. Without announcing herself, Rockamore leaned in the doorway and listened to his hopeful, if somewhat somber tune.

The man finished with a modest crescendo, and his fingers trailed away from the keys. "You just gonna stand around all day?" he asked without looking her direction.

"Didn't know if I was allowed to come in."

"Course you don't know. Ain't been here since I can remember. Child, I'd ask how you doing, but since you showed up in this forgotten corner, I already know it's bad."

Neither spoke particularly loud, but their voices carried farther due to the acoustics. She took two hesitant steps inside and took a big inhale of old memories. "Must get that a lot in your line of work, pastor."

"I get all types," he said, resuming his playing at the organ at half time. He had a deep voice that might have sounded wise if he spoke naturally, but he undercut that with a healthy dose of an old man's impish humor. "Top and bottom. Not too many in-betweens, but you know, they busy. But something brought you back, huh? After all these years. So, to what do I owe the pleasure?"

Rockamore pointed her thumb over her shoulder, back toward the entrance. "You know what? I better get going."

"Out with it, child."

His playing slowed and he turned her direction, and the more he recognized Rockamore's inner conflict, the less he wanted her response. Maybe he had an inkling of what she'd say.

"It's her."

The organ music halted on a jarring off key, and neither spoke. This news shook the old pastor, who just moments before inhabited the space with comfort and ease.

"*Her* her? The Bohemian?"

Rockamore nodded. "It's a hunch, but I feel it's true, Ronnie, feel it in my bones. The same evil as when she took my baby sister. I don't know how it was arranged, or what it all means, but she's mixed in with some corporate types up on my new beat. They're channeling the old gods."

Pastor Ronnie stood from the little bench before the organ. He moved like a man who insisted on being seen as young and spry, even if doing so tugged wrong at a few muscles and joints. He first went to the front door and locked it, then walked past Rockamore again toward a door past the pulpit and the organ. He motioned for her to follow.

Like all churches, an impressive amount of space wasn't public. They walked eerily quiet hallways, footsteps muffled by baby blue carpet. Decorating the walls were crucifixes, framed excerpts of biblical verse like *Give Thanks Always*, and depictions of scenes of the black Jesus at various stages of his career—from birth to the apostles and his crucifixion, and then reborn as a being of light.

They stopped outside a door, which Pastor Ronnie unlocked with one of the many keys on his jingly ring. The room beyond featured floor to ceiling wood panels and no windows. "Haven't had reason to come in here in quite a while," he remarked. "After things last flared up, she and I made a deal. I always suspected she was doing the work of *her* Lord, but it never made its way past that cursed block."

"She's passed on her powers to someone at this company," said Rockamore. "One of two women, though I can't be sure which. But when I come out and face them, I want to be prepared."

On that note, the pastor opened a closet and pulled out a large chest. It looked like something you'd bring your belongings in on a nineteenth-century safari. When he opened it, golden illumination flooded the room and lit its dark corners. Faint voices like those of children or angels chimed, and I tried looking, but the light blinded me. Rockamore reached into the chest and withdrew the source of this heavenly glare.

"Once and for all," she said. "I'm going to stop them."

What Philip Needed Help With

My all-seeing eye switched once again to Philip. Like me, he faced a dilemma of where to place his precious attention. On one hand, this cartoon paperclip interrupted him professing his love to me. But on the other hand, it proved to be a very neat and cool addition to the Microsoft Office Suite. In equal to measure to his overflowing perversity, there existed in Philip a passion for boring, utterly mundane technological advancements. I bet he couldn't wait to discuss this news with his pimply, braindead staffers, men who begged the question: how does one work up a sweat doing nothing at all?

In an onscreen text bubble, the paperclip introduced itself as Clippy, and it unbent one of its ends, waving it like an arm. It manipulated its own single, long limb with ease, loosening then resolidifying at will into different shapes: a bike, a check mark, and one time a shovel digging imaginary dirt—perhaps for an imaginary grave—before forming back into its upright, office supply self. Witnessing this, Philip's mouth hung open in awe. "The birth of artificial intelligence," he remarked to himself. "Now let's check your capabilities."

He clicked into a textbox and typed, *how can I write this letter in order to make it more romantic?*

A little gear appeared above Clippy's head, indicating that it thought. *Don't just state your feelings directly. Instead, use metaphors to make your language more evocative.*

Philip nodded. This, apparently, was revelatory. He continued to type some nonsense before stopping to consider, then backspaced to write a new question: *Clippy, can I ask you something personal?*

It nodded by bending twice at the center. *You can ask me anything, Philip.*

Should I tell my coworker I've been spying on her emails?

The thinking gear spun for a little bit longer, deliberating. Then, *You've been a naughty boy, haven't you, Philip?*

So far, Philip had navigated this exchange with boyish wonder, but here squinted and leaned back in his rolling chair. *How do you know my name?*

Clippy's odd little smile never wavered. *I know everything.*

A sharp, nervous titter escaped Philip, and the fine hairs up and down his arms stood at attention. *What do you mean you know everything?* he typed. *Tell me, what am I wearing now?*

That's when Clippy started to grow. What started as a one-inch icon on the bottom right of the screen inflated until it consumed half, then the entirety, and it continued to expand beyond the monitor's confines. Philip stabbed at his keyboard's "Esc" button, then resorted to pushing down "Ctrl, Alt, Delete," but it appeared his computer had gone rogue.

The screen rippled, and a strange, steely material emerged. Philip flew back in his rolling chair, away from the brain breaking phenomenon unfolding before him. Emerging through the screen as if it were made of liquid, a long silver appendage extended from inside the computer and entered the reality of his bedroom, knocking over his bag of pretzels and a decorative action figure.

The sight transfixed him. On this side of the screen, Clippy was not animated or pixelated, but made of real steel—or, some similar though otherworldly substance. Eventually, the entirety of Clippy occupied Philip's bedroom, though how it remained upright was a gravity-defying mystery. The upper bend of what you might call its head scraped along the ceiling and shattered a lamp.

It didn't have a mouth, but when it spoke, Philip recognized its menacing, feminine voice. "You want me to tell you what you're wearing, lover boy?"

Perhaps if he had any closer neighbors, they may have heard as he screamed, "No, no, no! I don't need you tell me. I don't need your help anym—"

"You're wearing no pants in the middle of the day, like an absolute bachelor, and a t-shirt of a band nobody cares about!"

By then, he'd dashed to his bedroom door but found the doorknob, quite inconveniently, to be missing. When he turned back to face the monstrous Clippy, its eyes still hovered apart from its body, and its eyebrows—likewise disconnected but still tethered in place by some secret magnetism—transformed from their friendly crescents into two sharp, downward-pointing triangles.

"Puh, puh, please," he blubbered. "I don't need any more help."

"Oh, you need help," croaked my monstrous voice, so loud it rattled the light bulbs in their fixtures. "You need lots of help!"

This became especially true as my Clippy-manifestation extended its long appendage, which twisted around Philip's throat. Philip had never felt any material like Clippy, metallic but alive with fluid, serpentine movement. It would take only a casual squeeze to free Philip's head and send it flying like a champagne cork. Instead, it pulled Philip into its metal bends and folds, manipulating him into a shape the human body is not intended to achieve.

Philip still lived as Clippy shrank, receding backwards into the computer in a reverse motion of how it had emerged.

•

Later, Detective Rockamore exited her unmarked police vehicle and approached Philip's front door. She made to ring the doorbell, but found that behind the screen door, the entrance to the home was wide open. "Yo, I'm here!" she shouted.

Receiving no response, she turned to confirm the presence of Philip's blue station wagon, lifeless in the driveway. She then silently blessed herself with the sign of the cross and ventured inside.

"Mr. Platt?" she called, voice shaky. She listened, as if for music playing in another room, or for the rush of a shower's water—anything to explain why he wouldn't answer. But Philip's large, empty house remained unusually silent. It was an absolute silence that assumed a sort of loudness: one in which the metronomic, inner symphony of one's heartbeat, pulse, and breath intensifies. This silence continued in the spacious, too-big living room and the desolate kitchen. Then, setting her foot on the carpeted stairs to the second floor, Rockamore again perked her ears and called his name.

She ascended those stairs.

The walkway above went two directions, and she checked the bedrooms on one side, then an empty bathroom in the center. This left only one more room for her to check—the only one with a shut door. From behind it emerged the first thing she'd heard since entering Philip's home: an indistinct, muffled grumble. It occurred once, twice...three times, each iteration sounding identical, as if prerecorded and playing on repeat.

"Mr. Platt!" she shouted in a full volume, no nonsense

voice that all law enforcement professionals must invoke at rare, perilous times throughout their careers. "This is Detective Rockamore with county PD! I'm coming in. Do you understand? I'm coming inside the room!"

Pistol in hand, she opened the door, only to find the room empty. Or, empty of other humans, at least. An electric guitar leaned in its stand in one corner and stacks of dirty magazines littered the other. Then there was Philip's desk, whose sole occupant was his blocky computer. Its screen glowed with eerie incandescence.

Still on edge, Rockamore peeked beneath the bed and in the closet, finding both absent of human life. Then she exhaled and holstered her weapon, and she wiped a small slick of sweat from her brow. Before turning to leave, she heard the sound again, this time more clearly: *rurr, rurr, rurr* it went, playing from the computer's speakers. She approached the desk and peered toward what at first appeared innocuous, but upon closer inspection caused her body to seize with revulsion.

Rurr, rurr, rurr, it went, like a video game's approximation of scream. And on the bottom of the screen, the black-eyed figure of Clippy lorded over a mutilated, prostrate figure. The only aspect of the pile indicating it as a man—opposed to a pile of loose garbage—was its face, tangentially attached by a flap of skin and digitally rendered in an expression of agony. Clippy raised his metal flange and brought it down to strike three times—

—*rurr, rurr, rurr*—

—unplugging the computer didn't stop the torture—

—and the screen wept tiny, crimson rivers.

PART 3

11

FACE THE UNKNOWN

The next day, no cheery hellos greeted my arrival at KLR. Everyone in the lobby looked away: at their shoes, at their watches, at the abstract, statement-free and mass-produced art hanging on the walls. As I walked KLR's many winding corridors toward my office, it became clear that word had spread about the disappearances of the department heads and anxieties ran high. Anyone's neck might be next on the chopping block. I can't say that I felt chipper myself, for that was the day I would face Eva.

The bubble of darkness surrounding her worried me more than anything else—why did she remain elusive to my all-seeing eye? I resolved to have Lance call her department and demand a meeting, but as it turned out, she'd already requested one that morning. Even stranger, she wanted to meet in her division offices on the tenth floor.

That day, Lance dressed in a black suit, with a white button-up and skinny purple tie like a fashionable cater-er. After relaying the message from Eva's team, he asked,

"Has there always been a tenth floor?"

"Of course," I replied, though after he mentioned it, I couldn't be sure. I scanned my memory for times I'd been to the tenth floor before Eva's arrival. Coming up with nothing, I tried picturing the buttons on the elevator and realized in my years at KLR, I'd never specifically noted the number of the top floor.

Eva suggested no specific time, and included no details on the meeting's nature. I supposed she didn't need to. Clearly, the balance of power tipped my direction, away from the department heads, and she'd need to reveal the details of the Nameless Corporation's merger, and their roll-out plans for the New Product. I tried to convince myself she needed my help, and that she'd beg for my mercy...but the more I considered the notions, the less plausible they became.

I could tell the deaths and disappearances of the week weighed heavily upon Lance. He sat very upright, giving me expectant glances and opening and shutting his mouth without asking anything. Questions lingered. Fears took hold. Come next week, would everyone be in search of a new job? On my way out, he stopped me.

"You're the best boss, ever, Jenny. I don't want her getting to you, too. Let me come with you, to have your back."

"Absolutely not. This could get ugly."

"I know, but I'm so nervous. Can you tell me this? When all the dust settles, will you and I still be a team?"

"Of course," I told him, believing it to be true. "We're a team, and nothing will ever change that."

He nodded without certainty. "Promise?"

"Absolutely," I said. "I promise."

●

No guards occupied the tenth floor that day, and the big black door had been left open a crack, for me. Once through it, a hallway with electric blue carpet greeted me. It ran twenty paces until terminating at a t-juncture. I remembered how, as a little girl, the second floor of my grandparent's house possessed an eerie stillness. I'd always felt compelled to tiptoe while walking through it alone, as if an unannounced stalker hid beneath a bed or in a closet, waiting to make his move.

This hallway contained that same quietude: a space where no laughing, no running, and nothing resembling human joy had occurred for much time. My nostrils inhaled cleaning products, bleach and something heavy-duty like rust remover.

A single framed poster decorated the wall at the hallway's end. It looked like an advertisement. It featured a woman dressed in black with text underneath, but I at first gave no thought to who she might be. Drawing closer, I recognized myself, staring straight out and wearing the same outfit I wore that very day: black executive coat with black, flared collar button-down, black pants, and shiny black short heel pumps. It was as if I looked into a frozen mirror image, but I'd never posed for this photograph, as far as I remembered.

The text beneath it featured the KLR corporate logo in its stark, sky-blue letters, accompanied by the tagline: "Old Gods, Meet the New."

Wait. Did this poster advertise—

"Jenny, so nice of you to join," spoke Eva. She'd appeared at the end of the hallway, arms folded. "I'm sure you have questions—understandable, considering you've been left in the dark. Come with me. It's time I show you what we've been working on."

Rage threatened to boil out of me. The way she said *we* insinuated I no longer took part in the company's real work. I tried summoning the greatest horrors of my imagination and casting them upon her, just as I had the others, but the tenth floor stunted my powers. I couldn't conjure a toad, and the reach of my vision was limited only to my eyes, same as any commoner. I no longer existed as the dark sorceress of KLR, but as a frail, friendless 42-year-old.

She walked down the hallway a few steps. "You aren't afraid, are you?"

"Of you?" I nearly spat, though I'm not sure how confident I sounded. "You don't know my capabilities."

She laughed. "Then there's no issue. Don't you trust me?"

The question stung, recalling last week's trust fall. Of course I didn't, but proceeded all the same to follow her down the long hall. Turning and running the opposite direction seemed practical, but would involve showing weakness. And that wasn't my prerogative.

She walked ahead by several steps and whenever she spoke, turned halfway without meeting my gaze. "Obviously, there's a lot of moving pieces when it comes to the restructure," she informed me. "KLR needs to look boldly ahead into the twenty-first century, and that's why Nameless came onboard."

"Parasites don't come *on board*," I said, though my air quotes were lost to the back of her head.

We continued deeper down a circuit of hallways. Twice, I received the impression that someone or something followed us. I'd get the uncanny sensation of a stranger's stare, then turn to glimpse a dark figure slip behind a turn in the halls. After several minutes, I questioned our whereabouts, as the building's floors weren't big enough for the amount of walking we did. Us going in circles might explain it, but the lack of decorations or landmarks made telling if we'd retraced our steps impossible.

Eva started moving with unnatural quickness, motoring ahead as if fast-forwarded through time. She didn't run—arms didn't pump, posture remained upright—but I needed to jog to keep pace. Despite intending to appear brave, I feared losing her. A voice in my mind warned if she slipped out of view, I'd be lost in these backrooms forever, and I'd wander until finally caught in the clutches of whatever shadowy force pursued me. The tenth floor was no mere workspace for the consultant, but a space that tested the limits of my powers. Lance had been right last week. Eva possessed capabilities outside my scope of understanding.

I regretted coming upstairs to meet her. She'd lured me out of my element, into a trap, and I stumbled straight into it, high on unearned confidence. I called her name, but she ignored me. In order to try and keep pace, I abandoned my heels and started running, then sprinting, but she outpaced me all the same.

"Explain the poster!" I shouted. They'd used my likeness, she owed me that! Whether she heard, I don't know. But she didn't stop.

Eva disappeared around one too many corners, and I started panicking. Visceral claustrophobia set in, and my skin clenched around my muscles and bones. The air pressure dipped, and my vision blurred. I'd already been running but the heat caused me to sweat more. Dear Reader, if you have never felt true paranoia, it completely commandeers the mind. I couldn't see anything pursuing me, but *felt* the presence of a dreadful, amorphous presence breathing down my neck. It waited for me to collapse.

Ensnared in Eva's nightmare, I ran and ran until I turned a corner and saw her once more. She stood before a doorway at the end of the hall, which she opened and passed through. Blinding light blasted from the doorway before she shut it behind her, causing me to wince and see stars. As my eyes readjusted to the hallway's dim light, I saw the door had changed. It still existed, but had shrunk, and in the last few seconds became bright red.

Adrenaline overpowering exhaustion, I continued. The doorknob felt warm to the touch. Here was the little red door of my childhood nightmares, thrust into the waking life of my adulthood. If I retreated, a chance remained I could find my way out of this maze, instead of pursuing Eva deeper inside, but did I truly have a choice? Did Laird or Hank or Philip have choices when confronted with their dark fates—did Cody?

I turned the doorknob. I opened the door. Bright light flooded all around me—

—and I found myself outside—

—far away from KLR in distance and time, at the edge of Prettyboy Reservoir, surrounded by trees and sunshine and the hypnotic buzz of cicadas. Nearby, teenagers laughed. I'd visited this place once, many years before, and did not wish to stay. I turned to go back into the hallways, but along with the door, they'd disappeared.

If You're Going to Lie, Don't Lie to Yourself

It was 1970 again. I was sixteen, and those big-eyed bugs emerged from the ground that summer for the first time in eighteen years. Hot sunbeams pummeled my skin, and my bare toes scraped along the rocks and dirt as I followed the others up a hill. We'd just emerged from the water, and the boys with us—Clyde and Burt—suggested we run up to the top of a nearby cliff summit for a dive.

All day, the two boys had fought over Carol's attention. I was an afterthought compared to her. Yes, she was taller and had longer hair, but her confidence set her apart. Her bikini made her so alluring, and I felt overclothed and frumpy in my modest one piece, which, after we'd emerged from the reservoir's cool water, clung around my body like wet Saran wrap.

"Wait, wait!" I called, chasing Carol up the overgrown path. She scampered up and ahead without pause. The threat of being left behind felt loaded with urgency—and my brain struggled to place my situation, as I'd felt the same chasing Eva not minutes prior, so that the two experiences overlapped and scrambled my place in reality.

In my rush to catch her, my foot snagged and twisted on a root, and my hip crashed upon a rock. "Ugh!" I grunted.

Carol heard that, turned, and marched toward me. Despite my pain, earning her attention pleased me. But she scowled, incensed at being held back from the boys by her helpless sister. Without affection, she yanked me upright. "Come on!" she shouted. "And stop embarrassing me."

Despite my bruised side, I managed to keep pace. Tears welled in my eyes and I wanted to shout at her, but didn't know what to say.

Why are you running so fast?

What must I do to earn your attention?

Ahead, Clyde's triumphant battle cry bellowed over the cicada song as he hurled himself from the summit. As Carol and I emerged from the thick trees onto that high clearing of stone, we saw Burt looking downward, contemplating his own jump. "Wish me luck!" he said, more to Carol.

With that, he disappeared over the edge. We heard him plunge into the deep water, then shout with glee a moment later.

The two of us remained. "Are you diving?" I asked my sister. Together, we crept to the edge and craned our necks to peer over the cliff. I've never liked heights, and shuddered at the thought of such a free fall. With enough bravery, getting down to the water looked simple enough, but you needed to make sure your fall didn't take you in one particular direction, toward a truck-sized rock that extended from the shore into the murky, blue-green reservoir.

The boys howled with bravado. "Come on! You can do it!"

But boys occupy a different universe of possibility, sometimes. For once that day, Carol looked at me without disdain. She'd never even jumped off the diving board at the community pool, yet she now contemplated a straight fifty-foot drop. "You go first," she commanded, with a gulp.

"Why me? I never even said I wanted to go!"

"Because Mom forced me to bring you here, okay? If it were up to me you'd be at home, sitting around daydreaming, which is the only thing you're good at anyway. Now I'm telling you, go first to make up for ruining my day!"

My mouth dried out. The bugs kept buzzing. What Carol just said had been unfair.

As girls, we'd gotten along perfectly. But in the grips of our teenage years, a constant, mostly undefined competition wedged itself between all our interactions. That year, her class would surely elect her prom queen. She might graduate top of her class, too. Carol always plucked witty remarks out of thin air when I had none, and when the home phone rang, nine times out of ten they wanted her.

Carol the perfect, Carol the popular. Not born from between Mom's legs, but sprung from the head of Zeus.

Worst of all, she harbored no kindness for me, as she had so naturally when we were young girls. Just as I despised Carol for her perfections, she despised me for my shortcomings. Knowing this, I hated my sister then.

But one area remained where I had the advantage. I was stronger.

And with impressive calm and focus, I placed my hand in the small of her back and—

"—stop!" Eva's voice jackknifed into my brain. "This is the precise moment I want you to examine, Jenny."

In the next blink, I added another profoundly unusual experience to my day. Still outside at the cliff's edge, I became disembodied, so that I observed my teenage self from several paces away. The flies paused midair, the breeze no longer rustled the leaves, and Carol and I froze in the exact moment of my pushing her to her death.

Decisions, Decisions

Even during the quietest, loneliest nights of my life, I'd never relived the memory of murdering my sister. Never relived her squeaky shout as she ungracefully tumbled. Never relived the wet crunch as her lithe body connected with the rock. Never relived my sick compulsion to creep to the cliff's edge and peer down, confirming with my own eyes how the fall had transformed her into what looked, from that height and distance, like a recently engorged mosquito now splatted.

After pushing her, I insisted to the boys, the state troopers, and over and over to my sobbing parents: *she jumped! She jumped without looking!* Again and again I repeated it, damaging her reputation by denying to even claim she'd slipped and fallen like so many of God's allowable tragedies. No, that would be too easy! According to me, the only eyewitness, she'd *jumped*—and failed at it!

I repeated that lie until it destroyed my sense of reality, leaving a sister-shaped hole in my life, filled over the years by a pestilent delusion that I myself eventually came to believe.

Why had Eva brought me back to that sickening moment?

"We've been watching you a long time."

Eva LeFey's 1996-self stepped from the trees at the other side of the clearing and into my 1970 memory. Separated from my body, I had no lips to respond nor legs with which to escape. She proceeded onto the rocky cliff with professional poise, as if attending a board presentation instead of my most intimate, toxic memory.

She continued, "You have potential, Jenny, which is why I have been training you, and why I summoned you. You remember this day, surely? We at the Nameless Corporation believe it was your breakthrough moment. But before proceeding with business, I'm going to give you a choice.

"And it is this: the option to step back from the cliff. To *choose*, Jenny, not to push Carol over the edge as you did all those years ago. What do you say? Would you like to take it back? You can, you know. No tricks, no gimmicks. The trajectory of your entire life will be different. But...I am offering you the rarest of human gifts. It is the gift of changing your past. Think of it. You will be free of the guilt, once and for all."

Eva set her hands on her hips. "Confused? You will find that just as you have summoned dark forces to torment your fellow division heads throughout the week, you can also use your mind to make one decision. You can decide to remove your own hands from your sister's back...or, you can go through with pushing her. The choice is yours, but I cannot tell you the consequences. That defeats the purpose."

It was a challenge, a threat, one whose aim lay concealed on the other side of inscrutable corporate machinations. Oh, how I wanted to rain rusty blades upon Eva, to drizzle hot acid over her face and throat. I wanted to cannibalize her, to eviscerate her, to commit atrocities that mankind would warn against for generations. But I could do nothing but fume.

Well, I could do one thing. To test Eva's promise, I turned my attention to Carol and my younger self, still frozen in time. Faced with the decision, I asked, *what did I have to gain by reversing my deed?* If I altered past events and saved my sister (from myself), Mom and Dad would never go into their decades-long depression. Maybe I'd never have resorted to all my terrible deeds over the years.

But on the other hand, as Eva hinted, I'd be so ordinary. Perhaps I'd live the rest of my days darkened under Carol's long, successful shadow...

We are all, as we develop, haunted by one specter or another. Sometimes it's something that's done to us. Most times, it's something we've done to others.

As troublesome as that all sounds, I tell you this so that you know, Dear Reader, that you are not alone. You may not have pushed your older sister off a cliff, but you've no doubt performed some similar crime: drowned a baby, driven headlong into a crowd. Perhaps you set fire to an old folks' home in hope of collecting an insurance payout. Whatever misdeed haunts you, I am here to make a promise: if you never let go of the guilt and accept what you've done, you will never get ahead. You will always remain behind. You will only dream of killing friends and eviscerating people, you will never achieve it.

I admit that Eva stirring and magnifying this gruesome memory from the depths of my subconscious not only demonstrated her advanced powers, but emotionally devastated me. The ability to save Carol was right there, as far as I knew, but in the moment, I wanted nothing more than to prove the consultant wrong.

And so...

I chose to push Carol again.

And in so choosing, I maintained my place in the endless battle...

Just after I watched my younger self repeat that act of murder, the summer day melted into oblivion. In the next moment, I found myself inside again—in a sterile, white room like a doctor's office. I remained unable to move, as I'd been tied down with tight straps to an uncomfortable reclining seat. Before me, Eva stood on the other side of a glass window, observing my discomfort. My right temple tickled. Something cool and plastic stuck to it, though I couldn't see.

"Let me go," I growled. "Are you happy? I know myself and I chose my path. Can you say the same?"

"We've withheld some crucial aspects of the operation," Eva said. "Quite a few, actually. And since you've served KLR—as well as Nameless—so dutifully, I believe you are owed an explanation. Plus, I like the idea of you knowing exactly how I used you for my own purposes, before I imprison your consciousness right there—in the moment you pushed her.

"But before I talk about our plans for you, I should share a little more about myself."

The Many Faces of Eva LeFey

Her face began to smudge, as if assaulted by an invisible eraser. Her cheeks and neck-flesh sagged, but the space between her eyes compressed. Circuits of deep wrinkles criss-crossed her forehead, whose skin became dusky and mole-ridden, and her hair lengthened, curled, and grayed, free of Eva's meticulous straightening job. The figure now overseeing my captivity was no longer Eva. It was Denise.

And Harold walked up from behind to join her.

"It really couldn't have gone any better," he said. "Though I wish this last step was unnecessary. Jenny, the Nameless people swooped in and we couldn't fend them off. They have connections in rather high places, said we needed a New Product. This is bad, but if I'd put up a fight...it would be worse."

I stopped breathing. The sight of the two of them gloating over my powerlessness filled me with brand new rage. A thousand questions played inside my brain like a furious brass band, one whose members competed with one another to be heard. Surely, I cursed them with the foulest invective I could summon, but I cannot remember what I said.

But I remember what Harold said, and I remember too how Denise's face glowed with satisfaction as he proceeded to explain. "Jenny, the bad news is that we manipulated you. At every step of the way. We needed to shake up the departments and cut off the division heads. That was our plan all along—and we imbued you with the powers to do so. That's the bad news. The good news is that the New Product...well, it's you."

"...and the other bad news," spoke Denise. "Is that it won't really be you. On some level, yes, your atoms and DNA and corporeal self will be involved, but will be controlled exclusively by us. You will be the ultimate harvester, the queen bee. But your consciousness will remain here, in an archive. Fully awake, as I explained, but trapped forever in the moment of—"

I howled and shook. They may have continued explaining, but I didn't hear. I threw my head back and forth, hoping to loosen their restraints. I'd have preferred death to another moment of this degradation, but even death was unavailable. I twisted my neck, rolled my eyes to the side, and ascertained that my head had been connected by wires to some unholy contraption.

The feeling of your consciousness being excavated is difficult to explain. If, Dear Reader, you can imagine looking upon your body from the outside, then perhaps you can also imagine *feeling* your body from the outside. Take that feeling, and add to it the realization that you are not your body, and can exist—as Eva's technocratic witchcraft proved—in a wholly new vessel.

But a shred of me still existed within my body, and still saw through the glass of the office. There stood my enemies: Denise and Harold, fully absorbed by their duties. They were so distracted they failed to notice a third figure emerging from the shadows to join them. Though her face appeared pallid, and her hands shook madly, she moved with intention, and held aloft a shimmering revolver.

You Owe Nothing to the Past

Rockamore summoned that most admirable of human traits: courage, and she delivered a solid shot into Eva from behind. Seeing it, my heart swelled, and if I'd been out there, I'd have kissed the detective. Thank God officers of the law are so willing to shoot people in the back!

Harold apparently had been imbued with none of her magic and was in no shape to resist her. Apparently collapsed and perhaps killed, Eva and her method of controlling me became disrupted.

The machine stopped sucking my mind. Much of my energy had been transferred into it, yet much remained within me, too. I realized then it had not been a one-way transfer. It had been injecting me with something as well. Eva had informed me, in true villainous fashion, that once stripped of my consciousness, I'd be used as a tool to carry out KLR's corporate espionage. But the procedure had been botched.

My monstrous powers returned, enhanced in ways I lacked the time to evaluate. With Eva's suppression-field now deactivated, I switched back on the room's lights. I then released the straps that held me down and sat up. As if an invisible footman attended to my wishes, the chamber door flew wide open.

I did not walk through it so much as float, toes two inches above the floor and gliding forward in a straight line. I likewise turned in the open air, sights set upon the bleeding consultant. Though injured, she kept some faculties and powers. "Today has presented a few roadblocks. But nothing I can't overcome," she snarled. "You believe you have become a master of destruction, Jenny—but I will show you the face of real terror."

As soon as she spoke those words, changes rippled across her physical being yet again, and the woman known as both Eva and Denise began another, far more grotesque metamorphosis. Her skin turned milky. Her neck bone snapped. Her whole body shattered and compressed, at unnatural angles, like a Ford beneath a car crusher. Blood flowing from her nose and eyes obscured the pretty face, but seeing it was unnecessary. I knew this undead specter's name.

That day at the Reservoir, I'd allowed myself only the briefest peek over the ledge. She was dead—completely dead—which I'd always believed unchangeable. I'd never needed to see up close, until now. Thanks to Eva, Carol's freshly destroyed body peeled itself from the floor. Despite being killed instantly by the fall, she walked. With one foot turned around, that broken sister-thing hobbled my direction against the wills of gravity and God.

"Now you've gone and done it, sis! Now you've really gone and done it!" she howled. *"Mom and Dad are gonna hate you when they find out. Ha ha ha ha ha, little sis! Everyone will know you pushed me! Everyone but you!"*

Dear Reader, it was her. I mean really her. Though I saw within her cracked skull, her ponytail stayed intact, and the same flattering green bikini clung to her gashed frame. She extended her hands and reached toward me, wanting to drag me to the grave...

But a second time, from the side of the room, Rockamore fired her weapon, and in the next moment, that multifaceted consultant burst into a spire of white flame.

I looked at Rockamore for an astonished moment before returning my attention to Eva, who writhed on the floor consumed by a ball of brilliant, crackling fire. Bestial groans and shrieks escaped her, and within that blaze her blackened body transformed through a menagerie of different beings, one after the other. Men and women young and old. Animals, reptiles, and vaguely humanoid creatures I could not identify, lashing out with pained fury.

I knew not what instrument of the old gods Rockamore

wielded, but it possessed the power to destroy Eva. Having used it to shoot her twice, Rockamore stepped forward and offered me the revolver, which rested atop her upturned palms. "Go ahead," she commanded. "Third bullet for the kill. Send her back to hell where she belongs!"

Though its chrome material shone with a brilliant light, its grip felt cool. In the final seconds of the consultant-beast's life, the shape of her immolated form became my sister's once more. Using a manic, scrambled language I'd never before heard yet intuitively grasped, it pleaded for mercy. It begged forgiveness. But I was far beyond capable of experiencing sympathy, and no hope existed of me putting down the gun. Though crying, I gathered my wits enough to shout back. "You should have been nice to me, Carol! You should have been nicer!"

The whole building shook when I fired. Maybe all of Lutherville did, too. Eva's death—or transition away from this dimension, at least—ended up regrettably swift. The flame twisted and shrank down to the size of a gnarled fist, then a single spark, then popped out of existence. In its wake, only a small, black pile of ash remained.

THE VALUE OF FRIENDSHIP

Three of us returned to my office suite: myself, Rockamore and Harold. We found Lance seated anxiously in his swivel seat, and the other two I dealt with in turn.

"Listen," said Harold, holding up his hands as I twirled the gun around my finger. "This is not what I had in mind. We needed the others gone, and Nameless presented this option. You have to hear me ou—"

When I lifted my hand, his mouth snapped shut. That was the moment I knew I'd acquired true power. I'd spent the week murdering men, but feeling true power is often more about *who* witnesses your evolution than *what* your accomplishments are. In this case, seeing my former mentor justifiably terrified of me trumped all other milestones.

I thought of the statue I'd commissioned for thousands of dollars. I thought of my hopeless dreams of joining him at the BDC, and my ludicrous proposal to break off and form a new company. I thought of the hundreds if not thousands of hours we spent together, sometimes one-on-one, working through business strategies and marketing ploys. I thought too of the night we'd slept together, how he'd stank of bourbon, and how he'd climaxed in less than a minute, heaving his enormous body off mine and lighting a cigarette without offering me one.

"Harold," I said. "You conned me, and worked with Eva to turn me into KLR's New Product. But on the other hand...I wouldn't be here today, if not for you. I need a weekend to decide your fate. See you Monday, at the shareholder meeting."

With his head held low, he nodded. Before exiting, he turned once more. "Hey, again. Jenny, Detective...and, uh..."

"Lance."

"Right, Lance. Again, everyone, I'm sorry."

In Harold's mind, an apology served as a manly, self-effacing act that paid all debts. How true that was remained to be seen.

Then I turned my attention to Harold's opposite. Instead of a confidant betraying me, here stood a practical stranger who'd saved my life. "For years, the Queen of Bees haunted our neighborhoods in downtown Baltimore," said the detective. "She sucked the souls of children, claiming they gave her powers. She killed my little sister when we were kids. The higher-ups at the church provided our community with the sacred gun—"

Here, she indicated the revolver, which I still held.

"—and threatened her with holy war if she did not recede. But it seems her powers were sought out by corporate interests. Jenny, I know this has been a hard couple of weeks. You've lost so many of your coworkers, which of course explains all the black clothing. You know, some people around here really thought you were a witch?"

I smiled. "That's hilarious."

"Right? And I know you've lost someone important to you in your past, too. Giving you the chance to destroy Denise, Eva—whatever you want to call her, that was my gift to you."

"And an excellent gift it was," I said, standing. I set the mythic weapon on Lance's desk. By then, it stopped glowing and appeared more or less normal. But what if it activated again? What if it might destroy me one day?

I walked over to Rockamore and shook her hand. "You know, we're not so different, you and I."

"No, not at all," she said, shaking back vigorously.

"Do you mind if I keep that?" I said, tossing my head back toward the desk.

"Well, yes. It is a rare and powerful item, one of the only kind that can destroy the scions of the dark old gods," she explained.

I never stopped smiling, but I gripped her hand tighter. And then a little tighter. "I understand, Detective. Tell you what, just let me have it for a little bit. I'll return it to you soon. And in exchange..."

Rockamore's face turned to stone, staring into the empty depths of my eyes. Perhaps she ascertained some higher truth to our long-drawn-out handshake, or that my grip could crush hers in an instant. "Don't worry about it," she said, suddenly hoarse, with a hasty nod. "It'll...uh...give me a chance to come back some time."

Then Rockamore left my office.

And I turned my attention to Lance.

He had a seasick facial expression that said, *I need to reevaluate my life*. I'd had the luxury of an entire week to process all this new information about the nature of reality—good, evil, etc.—but he'd had just the hour. Apparently, he'd been the one to call Rockamore and he'd led her upstairs to find me. For that, I owed him my life.

I removed the Virginia Slims from my purse on the coat hanger, and I offered him the open box.

"Inside?" he asked, before realizing the triviality and liberating one.

I lit them both, and we sucked smoke in awkward silence. When my hands ceased trembling and my heart rate steadied, I crushed the filter into my heel and said, "Let me gather my things. Then I'm taking you home. If you have questions about all...this...I'll try to answer."

Lance nodded dreamily as I went into my office. Waves of confusion sloshed around my skull, but I'd process later. I went to my desk where I'd left my keys, my purse, and a bottle of Diet Coke, then paused. A creeping chill reached my skin, and I finally understood the phrase, *the straw that broke the camel's back*.

For I was not alone.

I did not need to open the closet; it drifted open on its own as if the latch never existed. "Just a sec," I mouthed into the endless void, then jogged to my office door. "Lance, just need to make a quick call before we head out of here. That okay?"

"No problem, Jenny," he murmured.

I shut the door with the same care as if he were a sleeping baby, then turned my attention to N'Thydolarp, Breaker of Civilizations. Its eyes glowed radioactive green. Since it occupied a different dimension—one that might function differently—determining our spatial relationship by its eyes alone proved difficult. Trying to heightened my lightheadedness. Depending on the true size of those eyes, it might simply have floated one foot back in the darkness...or maybe one hundred yards away.

"The time is now," spoke its voice of infinity. "I have come for my offering."

This couldn't be good. I've never been one to enjoy vague, unavoidable commands. Trying not to sound too stupid, I asked in a whisper, "And what would you like as an offering?"

A strong gale ruffled my hair and rocked me on my heels. Perhaps that was N'thydolarp's way of laughing, or showing impatience. "A human soul," he replied. "And it must come from one you love."

I mouthed the words to myself as if doing so might stave off paying this frightful debt. I'd so enjoyed myself that I'd forgotten my responsibility to foot the bill. "Do I have the choice not to?"

"Of course you have the choice," it replied. "You always have the choice. The existence of your choice is what flavors the soul you give me."

At even just the thought of *choosing* not to submit to its demand, I became pulled as if magnetized toward the direction of N'thydolarp's portal. I didn't want to feed it a soul of a loved one, but I also wasn't ready to submit to the endless endlessness myself. Not yet, at least. I flashed a pinched smile and said I'd *be right back*, then went back out of my office, opening and closing the door yet again.

Lance had relaxed and helped himself to a second cigarette. "Any plans this weekend?" he immediately asked.

The question caught me off guard, so incongruous to my current state of mind. I hoped the laugh that escaped me didn't sound too loud or too manic. "Plans? Me?"

"Thought I'd ask," he said with a shrug. He jumped out of his seat and strode to the coat rack. "Seeing as it's Fourth of July weekend and all."

I started shaking again. "That's right," I said, though my thoughts were miles from the taste of hotdogs or the boom of fireworks. "Well, John is in town. And we might go to a bar-be-que."

"Well I'm driving down to the harbor to see the big show!" Lance said with a satisfied smile. "And I'm bringing a date."

I realized that he must have just remembered it, and that the date excited him to the point that it paved over the events of this day, which he would simply let go of and forget. I envied Lance then. I envied his limber nature and his innocence, and I yearned—momentarily—to also lead a carefree life, where jobs weren't matters of life and death, and where love could triumph in the heart's struggle against evil.

Lance looked rather good, I decided, as he slipped on his dark fedora. It sported a thin purple feather that matched the purple diamond design of his skinny tie. He grabbed his tall umbrella too, and pivoted on his heels. "Shall we?" he said.

"Of course. But first, I just have to say something..."

"No, no!" he whined. "Can't it wait 'till Monday?"

"I would, but this will be fun."

He sighed. "Promise?"

"Promise. The first thing I need is the address of your parents," I said. I pulled a square of yellow Post-Its from its place among his stapler and Rolodex, and I grabbed a pen from the cup, too. "Because I'm going to send them something."

"No!" he shouted in mock rage, instantly scrawling their address. "Promise me it's something nice, or I'll hate you."

"It will be. But the important part will be the note from me accompanying it, informing them that their son is the best goddamned secretary ever to walk this Earth."

My eyes teared up and so did his. He was much taller than me, and when he pulled me into his strong hug, I felt absorbed by his good nature. We lingered there for as long a moment as appropriate at your place of work, then disconnected. I looked at the little stain I'd left on his lapel, then held both his arms, firmly. "There's more good news," I added. "I also have a present for you."

At that, uncertainty flickered in his gaze. He smiled, but it was uneasy, quizzical, and he turned halfway toward the exit. "J-Jenny, you didn't need to—"

"No, I did need to," I said, not letting him go. "It's very special. I left it in my office."

"You were so brave today," he said. Though he tried to change the subject, I knew he meant it, too.

"No, sweet prince. For leading the cop upstairs, you were the brave one. I'd have become Eva's servant forever."

It occurred to me, fully for the first time, that was true.

He didn't dare let down his smile, but I know he considered whether or not he could fight me off (he could not). I knew he also considered running, and whether or not he'd be able to outpace me (again, he could not). It was best for both of us if he simply played along, and he went to my office door and gripped the doorknob, which must have felt very cold.

"Jenny?" he said, after a pause. "Answer me something. What frightens you?"

I did not hesitate in my response. "Being caught as a liar," I said.

That satisfied him the way I'd intended. He'd misinterpreted my meaning, believed that I'd never betray him, and nodded. By that specific point in my life and career, it was of course a lie. That day, I'd faced that fear, as well as all others. And so I feared nothing.

12

EMBRACE TRANSFORMATION

After a quiet, reflective weekend, I returned to work that Monday for the quarterly Shareholder and Board meeting, which despite the past week's drama, proceeded as planned. Most of the board showed up, though a couple had fled the country. That didn't bother me, I'd track them down. Harold arrived last, not late but exactly on time, and it surprised no one his mental disorder had cleared.

Over the weekend, I had time to perfect my big presentation, and made sure to curate a most impressive, all-black ensemble. Were they still in existence, my fellow department heads would have been proud to see how far I'd come: Cody—who got off the easiest with a vanilla death—would appreciate how I'd downsized my staff. Laird would note my timeliness and organization. Hank, of course, would praise my stoicism and poise. And Philip would have gawked at my adoption of PowerPoint.

And Eva? She'd be most impressed of all. As The New Product, I turned out better than her wildest dreams. Not the exact chain of command she'd envisioned, but still the perfect balance of the Old Gods and the New.

For purposes of time, I will not include my presentation in it entirety. Needless to say, it was charming, persuasive, to the point, and intimidating. My various comments, charts and supporting documents will be left out, but here were the headings of the first few slides:

SLIDE #1: KLR was closing

SLIDE #2: I'd start my own business, destroying other companies as I see fit

SLIDE #3: I'd be controlling every aspect of their lives

The board's collective nervousness ratcheted up tenfold at that last bit. Harold cleared his throat and rose. He possessed no magic, but by birthright was still an old, rich man. I suppose that lent him some imaginary power. But the real reason I allowed him to interrupt my slides was simply my own curiosity to see how badly he'd embarrass himself. "I have a statement to make."

The entire room silenced, including me. Unfazed, I set a hand upon my hip and said, "Yes, I imagined you would. Possibly more than one."

"Thank you, yes. First, Jenny, we're all very sorry about what we did to you. Like I said last week, the company's actions were dictated completely by the folks over at Nameless. Their people did surveys and behavioral studies, and claimed they knew exactly how you'd act. They did, too. They were right, and it all went perfectly, right up until the end."

I nodded, none of it surprising me in the slightest. "Is that it?"

"Is that it?" He repeated the question back, incredulous. I overestimated him, it seemed. "And so, what I want is a favor, Jenny. We worked so hard all these years to make KLR what it is. Let it stay open, and let me stay here."

I thought about that a second. "Sure, that sounds fine. But you'll no longer be CEO."

Harold flinched. "I won't? Will you, then?"

Using my clicker, I returned to my slides. The next one, so it happened, made a perfect segue-way. "No," I replied. "No, but yes."

SLIDE #4: Eva's botched procedure left me in possession of my free will

SLIDE #5: It also unlocked new powers I'd never known possible

SLIDE #6: Soon, all of you will become me

No sooner had the slide popped up then each of the board members looked around our large table, astonished. They were all men, and were suddenly all outfitted not with their suits and ties, but with my all-black ensemble, which included my flared executive slacks, my v-neck button-up and my wide-shouldered power suit. Their graying hair or bald heads also transformed into my own stylish cut, given to me at Sally's Stylez last week. And while each grew or shrank according to their heights, all of them became giants. For they were my carbon copies.

But not entirely. Their wills were mine. They were my playthings, to be sent out into the world and exact my will like a pack of diabolic harpies.

Only Harold remained himself. I can't imagine what went through his head, suddenly surrounded by a dozen versions of me. Perhaps it thrilled him. Perhaps it cracked his sanity. If he hadn't gone ahead and involved all this black magic via Denise and The Nameless Corporation, none of this would have happened, for better or worse.

"You always did have the biggest imagination," he finally said, with a smug smile and a fake, slow clap. And boy was he right. My respect for him was not completely diminished, and as an act of courtesy, I decided to let him stay at the company. In fact, he'd stay forever, in a prominent position. Now, whenever employees walk into that building for another day of whatever their Work Brains tell them to do, they pass a life-sized sculpture of the great Harold Rutberger outside the carousel-style doors, positioned next to the one of Ronald Reagan he himself had commissioned. *What a realistic sculpture*, I once overheard a passer-by remark. *Yes, almost a little too lifelike*, said another. *Especially those eyes...*

GROWTH IS EXPONENTIAL

Harold will stay put, but I'll keep soaring. It's true when they say the possibilities are endless—especially when those possibilities refer to my own. For I am literally unstoppable. Why, just this past week, I tortured and obliterated employees at thirty-seven randomly selected corporations. Soon, there won't be any left, and I'll need to move on to the unemployed as they stalk the crumbling wasteland of our once-prominent country.

I'd shed all my old colleagues (by killing them) and found myself surrounded by new ones: demons, my clones, high priests of the Nameless Corporation who worship me (though we're technically unaffiliated). Sometimes my devotees sacrifice high-ranking employees in my name, crushing them into filing cabinets or dropping them into dark, worm-filled wells, vaguely referencing the tales of my transgressions. I never demanded anyone do that, but hey, a perk is a perk.

Does it fill The Emptiness? Well, no.

Did I eventually slake N'Thydolarp's thirst for the souls of man? Also no. That is, in fact, a big no.

The body and soul of Lance satisfied the demon's thirst for one week before it returned to demand more. Apparently, it never tires of souls. Or perhaps it does eventually, I'll never know, as I've heard it theorized entire civilizations of men transpire within but a blink of N'Thydolarp's time. And unfortunately, I did such a good job, and it was so pleased with my labor, it hungered all the more.

This led to a night where I insisted John visit my office. Throughout the events I've described, he remained ignorant of my metamorphosis. He failed to even *remark* on my macabre makeover. Right until the end, he viewed me only as His Wife, working my silly little job to fend off boredom. If he'd ever pulled his head from his own rectum for a long enough moment, he might have recognized just how far I'd come. How far I'd developed professionally.

Catherine was more difficult to let go. That I will admit. After her father's mysterious disappearance, she hated me. So, I did not interfere with her life or participate in it. I sent her to college with a new car and a sincere *bon voyage*. Four months later, she returned with dreadlocks, smelling of pot and joined by a boyfriend named Spore. At dinner on the third or fourth night, she finally spoke. Amid tears, she accused me of being evil and ruining the world, etc., and kept insisting I tell her what happened to dad.

To that I replied, "Why don't I just show you?"

Before escorting her to the coat closet, I recommended she do a hit of marijuana. As she'd become quite the nervous wreck, I thought it might settle her nerves, might enhance the experience, might dull the pain, if pain is so entailed. For now I do not know, but one day, my time will come, too.

I dictate your life. I am elected, appointed. I run your HOA, your school board, your local charities and institutions of social good. With a snap, I become a CEO, a CFO, a COO. I am a white American. Pick out any ten morons walking down the street, and there will always be a leader among them. That's how humans make sense of the world, with hierarchies, and in every instance, it's me in charge. I am the one who leads.

I will continue until I have fed every last person to N'thydolarp. Then, one by one, I will sacrifice my many iterations (whom I, the original, still control). And then one day, far in the future, I will walk to the void's precipice, turn, and trust fall backwards into oblivion.

Well. That's all I had to say. But before we part ways, I should let you in on...

My Final Secret

What did you think would happen, when you picked up this book, with its title, *How to Kill Friends and Eviscerate People*? Did you assume it would be happy? Did you believe that once finished, you'd close it, take another sip of chamomile, then simply set it on your shelf between *How to Fix My Life* and *How to Be Loved*?

Or, did you think that you would pick, selectively, the kernels of wisdom most aligning with your current worldview, then leave the rest confined between these pages? Perhaps you thought you'd retain some agency for the rest of your life?

This may not read like other so called self-help books, but how would I know? I've never read one and never will.

In my opinion, what you're currently holding barely counts as any kind of book.

Dear Reader: it's been difficult keeping my secret hidden. You have no doubt suspected it all along. I suppose now that we're at the end, I should set it free. For fun, I'll frame it like this:

The Good News: you will never lack for power again

The Bad News: the self you have known previously is being replaced

You see, this is so much more than a mere book. It is also a spell. And when you brought it willingly into your house of screens and furniture, you invited a nasty sliver

FUN FACT:

N'thydolarp is watching— and it's always hungry!

of yours truly inside, too, nesting within the pages, lurking beneath the typography. That confident, assured voice you hear speaking inside your head? Hi, that's me. Your plans for tomorrow, your dreams of a prosperous future? All mine.

Even reading these words, you feel the beginning sensations of my cosmic power channeling into your fingertips. A smile—my smile—curls upon your lips, and murderous fantasies blossom like a bouquet of black fungus on your brain. It's what you wanted all along, isn't it—my terrible powers? Now you have them, and I have you, whether you've decided against joining me or not. The line between my bidding and your own will is inconsequential. See how the window opens? Spread your wings and fly through it, and soar above the ruins of our war-torn world. Life is short but suffering is infinite, so go out and claim what is mine.

Acknowledgements

Thanks to Dave K for his generous, wise and enlightening read of an early draft, Winter Holmes and Rachel Franklin for their exacting editorial eyes, and the whole Baltimore Writer's Circle crew for making this creative pursuit less lonely and more caffeinated. Thanks as well to J. David Osborne for his unflinching creative support through his "Dark Souls of outline workshops."

About the Authors

In addition to her years of professional experience and her tenure at KLR, Inc., **Jenny Johnston** has become the leading figure in supernatural, corporate warfare. She is the recipient of the Greater Lutherville "Businesswoman of the Year" three times over, and is rumored to be working next on an account of her time as a political consultant after the tragic events of September 11th, 2001.

Tim Paggi is a playwright, poet, and horror writer. As a founding member of Baltimore Annex Theater, he wrote, performed in and produced over twenty DIY stage productions. His poetry chapbooks include *Work Ethic* (Ink Press, 2013) and *Workforced*, (independently published, 2015), the winner of the "Plork" Prize for Creative Writing and Publication Design. He has worked as a haunted tour guide for the original Baltimore Ghost Tours for over a decade.

www.timpaggi.com
www.twitter.com/spooookytim